A Match for the Matchmaker

Escape to Ireland Book 4

Michele Brouder

Editing by Jessica Peirce

Book Cover Design by Rebecca Ruger

A Match for the Matchmaker

To God be the Glory.

Chapter One

Carrie Fields heard the familiar rap of her editor's knuckle on his office window and looked up from her desk. Once he had her attention, he waved her over. Carrie glanced at the hard copy she'd been marking up, put down her red pencil, and reached over and turned off the police scanner she kept beside her as she worked.

She stood up, pushing her chair back, and started toward her boss's office. As she did, she stubbed her toe on the leg of her desk and half-hopped, half ran the rest of the way. Peter, over at the sports desk, laughed. "Hey, Fields, what's up? First day with the new feet?" He threw a mini basketball into his desk hoop and stage-whispered, "He shoots, he scores!" adding a roar of the crowd for effect.

Carrie ignored him, wincing. Her big toe throbbed. She wobbled on her heel into Sam's office.

"Sit down," he said, indicating a chair.

Carrie sank into the office chair with relief. Briefly, she wondered if the toe was broken. That would be just her luck. And it wouldn't be the first time.

"Carrie, I've got a special assignment for you," Sam said.

Carrie sat up straighter, feeling the excitement and anticipation of a new story. Carrie loved her job as a crime reporter. Her boss, contrary to the stereotypes she'd harbored when she first started at the paper, was as kind as her grandfather. And while some days the stories she covered broke her heart, there was never a doubt in her mind that she'd made the right career choice.

Sam closed the door behind her and sat down at his desk. "I haven't told the rest of the staff yet, but Barbara had a heart attack last night."

Carrie's eyes widened and her hand flew to her mouth, her sore toe forgotten. Barbara Edson had been reporting for the *Philadelphia Chronicle* longer than anyone else there, specializing in human interest stories. She was not only a combination colleague slash den mother who had served as a mentor for Carrie, she was also a great journalist.

"Is she going to be all right?"

"Steve said they put a couple of stents in, but she should be fine," Sam explained with a shrug, referring to Barbara's husband.

"What can I do?" Carrie asked.

"Barbara is in the middle of working on a piece about dating in the 21st century, and I need you to fill in for her."

"Okay," Carrie said with a slight hesitation in her voice.

"She was supposed to leave for Ireland tomorrow to interview a traditional matchmaker."

"A matchmaker? Really?" Carrie repeated, blinking. "I thought they only existed in the movies."

"Just an interview with the matchmaker, is that it?"

Sam opened a folder and went through a sheaf of papers. "She was going to do a write up on the festival itself as well as interview some of the couples who met their matches at the festival."

"Okay," Carrie said nodding. She'd go through her colleague's notes and put her own spin on things.

Sam nodded, tapping a pencil against his desk. "Hard to believe with all the online dating nowadays, but apparently there's still a few of them out there. This one operates in some remote part of Ireland, and apparently he's quite successful."

Carrie raised her eyebrows. He? A man in the role of a traditional matchmaker? She was intrigued.

"I know right?"

"Who will cover me while I'm gone?" Carrie asked. She hadn't been at the crime desk that long.

"I'm going to divvy your workload between Bob and myself."

"When do I leave?"

"I was hoping you could leave tomorrow. The deadline and all that. Martha is working on your ticket right now. Barbara was going for two weeks."

"Two weeks, great," she said. She didn't know much about Ireland—Home of Guinness beer? It rained a lot? Yep, that summed it up—but she was looking forward to exploring a new place.

Her boss slid a folder across his desk toward her. "Here's the information Barbara has pulled together. The matchmaker is expecting her, but I'm sure you can sort that out when you get there."

Carrie nodded. "Sure." She opened the folder to take a cursory glance. There were notes on lined paper in Barbara's neat, looping handwriting, which brought a smile to Carrie's face. She sure hoped Barb was going to be okay. Beneath the notes were photocopies of an article that had appeared in *The*

Kilcornan Weekly, an Irish newspaper. Carrie froze when she spotted a grainy photo of the matchmaker. She pulled out the article and studied the image. She froze.

Sam's voice jarred her out of her reverie. "What's wrong, Fields? You look like you've seen a ghost!"

Carrie smiled weakly and snapped the folder shut, covering up the photo. She had indeed seen a ghost.

The matchmaker was Mick Foley. Her husband. Whom she hadn't seen since he'd left her more than ten years earlier.

CHAPTER TWO

"ROSEMARY, YOU KNOW I can't stand giving interviews," Mick Foley said to his sister, having the same conversation they had every year at the start of the festival. "I've agreed to give *one* interview this year to an American newspaper and as far as I'm concerned, I'm good now for ten years." He returned his attention to the *New York Times* crossword puzzle.

"I know that, but you should rethink that decision," she said. "When is that American journalist coming to town?"

Mick glanced at his sister. "I think any day now. Barbara something is her name. I'll have to check my emails again."

"What made you agree to this interview?" Rosemary asked.

Mick frowned, not quite sure how to explain it. "I don't know. She came across as nice in her emails."

When Barbara from the *Philadelphia Chronicle* had reached out to him, she'd revealed in the first line of her email how his mother, Bridie Foley, had set her up with a fellow American more than twenty-five years earlier. It was almost like a personal reference from his late mother. Despite his desire for privacy, he felt he couldn't refuse the woman.

Rosemary scoffed. "Hope she doesn't turn out to be Attila the Hun."

They were in her cozy café in the west of Ireland, in the little rural village of Kilcornan. Rosemary's apron was covered in flour as she made a batch of scones. Like her brother, she was tall and solid. A red bandana covered her dark hair. Mick sat on a high stool on the other side of the island, drinking a cup of tea.

Rosemary was older by only two years, but she sometimes behaved as if she were his mother and not his older sister.

"You're like an old man with your crossword puzzles and aversion to social media and technology," Rosemary griped. "You'd never know you were thirty-two years old."

Mick focused on eight down of the crossword and frowned.

"Hear me out about doing more interviews," Rosemary said, kneading dough on the lightly floured surface in front of her.

He sighed, looking up at her. There was no choice in "hearing her out." Rosemary was always going to say what she wanted or needed to say. He took a sip of his tea and waited.

"With the festival starting the day after tomorrow, the publicity would be good. You can't argue with the figures, Mick," she started.

Rosemary was right about not being able to argue about the figures. Over the last few years, the attendance numbers for the matchmaking festival had been slightly declining. It was likely due to the rising popularity of online dating. And fewer people meant less money for the town. The town depended on the revenue from the festival as it had for the last one hundred years.

Mick was a lover of history and a believer in tradition. All this new technology did not impress him. Rosemary spoke of using Facebook and Instagram to drum up business. He didn't even know what Instagram was, let alone how to use it to drum up business. Both her watch and her phone were hi-tech. His watch had a second hand, and he was still using a flip phone.

"Did I tell you that Charlotte Connors rang yesterday?" she said, using a fluted cutter to punch out shapes in the dough.

Mick rolled his eyes. Charlotte Connors was a blogger from Cork City who first arrived at the festival a few years back, looking for love.

Charlotte Connors was one of the reasons Mick no longer gave interviews. In a weak moment, he'd allowed Rosemary to talk him into agreeing to give an interview to Charlotte, describing the blogger as a social influencer. It turned out that Charlotte had about as much influence as Mick. And since then, he couldn't get rid of her. She'd become a regular at the festival, much to Mick's chagrin.

"She wanted to know if you had a girlfriend," Rosemary teased, laying the scones on a baking tray.

Mick groaned. It seemed Charlotte's main mission in life was to convince him that she was his soul mate.

Rosemary stopped what she was doing. "What's wrong with Charlotte? She seems very nice, actually. You could do a lot worse."

Mick shook his head. "She just doesn't tick the boxes for me."

"Maybe you need to get new boxes," Rosemary suggested.

"No. Besides, she has ideas of being a partner in the match-making business."

Even Rosemary paled and dropped the subject. The Foleys were very serious about their matchmaking legacy.

Charlotte had wanted to know his secrets to matchmaking, insisting that she could assist him with it. But there was no secret. Or even a set of rules. The truth was, Mick didn't even know himself. His grandmother had explained that it was a gift. That it related to the senses and wasn't an exact science. And no one had been more surprised than he when "the gift" had passed over his sister and landed on him.

You could just look at one person and another and you knew that they needed to be together. Mick went through the appearance of paperwork and questionnaires for people to fill out as a matter of form. But he barely cast a glance at them. He observed people, spoke with them, and watched how they interacted with others. He liked talking to the people as individuals and then as a couple. That's how he set people up. It was something that couldn't be explained. But try and tell that to someone like Charlotte Connors. She wanted a formula for success and Mick didn't have one.

"Anyway, while we're on the subject," Rosemary continued. It was her segue into bringing up a potentially prickly topic. Mick braced himself. "It is a matchmaking festival, you know."

"I do know. We run it," he said. It was the tradition for the town matchmaker to be in charge of the festival, and Mick was also the director of all the activities and events.

"What I mean is, there are going to be a lot of single women there and, you know . . ." she said, her voice trailing off.

"No, I don't know," he said, but knowing exactly where she was heading.

"It's just that you should try to find someone for yourself," she said.

When he didn't say anything, she carried on. Rosemary would say her piece. It was usually best to just let her get on with it.

"Sometimes I worry about you," she said. "You brood too much and listening to all those sad Irish songs does you no good. Thank goodness you don't drink—that would be a lethal combination."

He agreed with her about drinking. Their father had done enough drinking for everyone.

"Are you depressed?" she asked.

If it wasn't such a serious subject, Mick would have laughed. "No, of course not. I just enjoy listening to sad Irish songs."

Rosemary rolled her eyes.

It was true. He did like to listen to traditional Irish songs. And they weren't all sad. Though some of them were. It made him think of times past. But he wasn't depressed. There was a word for it. A Portuguese word that he happened to like very much:

Saudade.

They were interrupted by a knock at the back door. Rosemary glanced at the clock up on the wall. "That's Dennis. You could set your watch by him."

Mick wanted to kiss him for his perfect timing.

Rosemary wiped her hands on a towel, pulled off her bandana, and opened up the back door to let in Dennis, her produce guy. He carried in a crate of lettuce. "Morning, Rosemary, how are you? Got the weekly delivery." He laid the crate at the end of the table. He nodded to Mick. "Morning, Mick."

Mick nodded hello.

"Let me help you, Dennis," Rosemary said, and she followed him outside to his truck. The two of them returned carrying crates of colorful fruits and vegetables. Rosemary shouldered her crate and set it down next to the others on the table.

Dennis regarded her with admiration. "You're a powerful woman, Rosemary."

"That I am." She laughed.

"Now, will we go over the order for next week? I can ring you later if you'd prefer," Dennis said. Dennis was the owner of his own wholesale produce business, and although the top of his closely shorn head barely reached Rosemary's chin, he seemed unable to take his eyes off her.

"Nah, I've got the list for you now, right here," Rosemary said, pulling a folded piece of paper from her apron pocket.

Dennis took it from her, looking oddly disappointed. Mick studied him.

"Are you sure you only want one crate of tomatoes?" he asked.

"One will be fine for now, Dennis," Rosemary said, turning her attention back to her scones. "I'll see you next week."

Dennis watched her for a moment before heading back out the door. Mick grinned. Dennis's crush on Rosemary was obvious to him, but his sister remained clueless. Dennis was a sound guy.

Once the door slammed shut, Rosemary said, "Now, back to what we were talking about."

"Charlotte Connors."

"You need to tell her you're not interested," she said as she put the baking tray full of scones into the industrial oven. "Don't lead her on."

"I've told her. Several times. She thinks I'm playing hard to get."

She did not hide her look of surprise. She appeared thoughtful and asked, "Will I talk to her? You know, woman to woman, he's not that into you, that sort of thing?"

Mick was aghast. "No!" The last thing he wanted was for his sister to fight his battles.

Besides, he'd already been in love once. But that had been a long time ago.

Mick was just at the end of the row of shops when Maeve O'Donovan stepped out from her place of business. The original marquee above the entrance read simply, "O'Donovan's, est. 1892." The shop had been started by her grandfather, and Maeve continued to run it along with her twin sister, Millie, despite the fact that the two of them were shoving on to ninety. O'Donovan's sold an odd assortment of things from dish racks to clocks to fine china teacups and "all sorts of fripperies," as Mick's mother used to say. The twins had been contemporaries of his grandmother. They'd also spent over four decades operating a similar shop on the Isle of Wight but had retired back in Ireland and taken over the family business.

Mick stopped for her, nodding in greeting.

"Mick! Hold up," Maeve called out. "This is going to be your year! I can feel it in my waters."

"Maybe my numbers will come in for the Euro Millions," he joked.

"Seriously, Mick," she said, concern washing over her features. "It's time you settled down. Your mother and grandmother wouldn't want you to be alone. There's someone for you out there. I think we're going to need to stir the pot a bit."

"Not necessary." He smiled kindly. "I'll find my own match, thanks."

"Aw go on, you know your gift doesn't work for you," Maeve challenged him. "That's what your grandmother told me a very long time ago."

"Still, I'd like to have a say in the matter," he insisted. "Where's your partner in crime?" he asked, referring to Millie.

"She's a wee bit under the weather," Maeve told him.

Mick frowned. "Do you need the doctor to come out?"

Maeve waved him off. "Of course not, nothing a shot of whiskey can't cure." She slapped her forehead. "I've got to remember to pick up a bottle of whiskey."

"Don't forget," Mick teased. The O'Donovan sisters were known to take a shot of whiskey for whatever ailed them.

Maeve was not to be deterred. "Maybe Millie and I could get a list of candidates together and you could choose from that."

He tried not to look horrified; he knew she meant well. But lining up women like cows in a mart was not how he'd imagine anyone would want to pick a mate.

He bid her goodbye, asking her to send along his regards to her sister, and headed back to his walkabout.

Poor Maeve. She had no idea that Mick could never get married. Ever.

Chapter Three

"Are you sure David doesn't mind you leaving for two weeks?" Carrie asked as they stood in line waiting to board their plane. She'd asked her best friend, Kathy, if she wanted to tag along. Her friend had jumped at the chance.

Kathy snorted. "David? He probably won't even notice I'm gone until day three or four, when he's out of clean laundry!" Kathy sighed and then grumbled, "He'll probably throw a party once he reads my note."

Carrie's eyes widened in surprise. "You didn't tell him you were going to Ireland for two weeks? You just left him a note?" She knew that Kathy and David were having some problems, but she'd figured it was just a bump in the road. They'd been living together for three years.

Kathy shrugged. "We hardly see each other anymore. He's working all these extra shifts. Why, I don't know, because we always manage to pay all our bills."

"Have you asked him?" Carrie asked, pointing out the obvious.

"It's hard to ask him anything when he's never there! And when he is home all he wants to do is sit around, drink beer, and watch any game with a ball in it."

David was a detective with the Philadelphia police department. Carrie was sad to hear their relationship was in trouble; she liked David, and she liked him for Kathy. It just proved to her that no one knew what really went on between a couple except the couple themselves.

As they approached the airline agent at the gate, Carrie pulled out her boarding pass and passport for presentation, and her friend did the same.

Kathy had managed to get on the same flight as Carrie but not in a seat in the same row. As Carrie stowed her carry-on in the overhead compartment, she said to her friend, "I'll see you in Shannon."

Kathy smiled and nodded, heading toward her seat further back on the plane, her carry-on trailing behind her.

Once situated, Carrie stared out the window at the airport workers wearing headphones and orange hi-vis jackets. From below, she could hear luggage being loaded with a continuous stream of thumps.

She was soon lost in thoughts of Mick Foley. The last time she'd seen him, she was nineteen and he was twenty-two. She'd be lying if she said she hadn't thought of him over the ensuing years. For a long time, she'd expected him to walk back through her door, but it had not happened. *Won't he get a surprise when I walk through his door after all this time*, she thought ironically. She had yet to contact Mick and tell him that she was coming in Barbara's place. Indecision had plagued her on this. Professionally, she should have informed him of the change. But emotionally, she wanted to have the advantage. In the end, her heart had won out.

Carrie leaned back in her seat and thought back to the time when she'd first met Mick. She'd been a sophomore in college, and he'd graduated from college in Ireland but had a visa to work the summer in Cape Cod. She'd been bookish and nerdy and let her friends drag her to a restaurant out on the Cape. Mick had been tending the bar. Immediately, she'd been attracted to his impossibly tall and solid build and his mop of dark hair. But his accent! That was an adventure in itself. Carrie squeezed her eyes shut at the memories of it. He was always so unfailingly polite. It got to the point where she was only going into the bar to see him, and eventually he confided in her that he was planning on renewing his visa as he wasn't ready to leave America yet.

One night, she arrived at the bar and it was as if his personality had changed. He was quiet to the point of being sullen. She tried several times to engage him in conversation. Finally, at the end of the night, she gave up, slid off her barstool and headed for the exit. He called out after her. Even now, after all this time, she could still remember the way the goosebumps erupted over her skin at the sound of her name on his lips. He asked if he could talk to her. Up close, his eyes were dark and serious, and he looked as if he had the weight of the world on his shoulders. He was closing up and once everyone left, it was just him and her. Alone. She hoped he would ask her out.

He came out from behind the bar with two Cokes, then proceeded to pour out his story: he was returning home to Ireland, as his visa renewal had been denied. Carrie was surprised. She hadn't expected this. Her mind worked furiously. All she could think about was that if he returned to Ireland, she'd never see him again. Her heart felt as heavy as lead. Mick admitted to being depressed about it. He had tried in vain to appeal the decision.

After an awkward silence, Carrie clapped her hands and blurted out, "I have an idea! We could get married and then you'd be able to stay."

Mick looked horrified and Carrie tried not to let her feelings be hurt, but it was almost impossible. She knew she wasn't going to win any beauty pageants, but she still had a lot going for her.

"I can't ask you to do that," he protested. "It's illegal, first of all."

Carrie had shrugged. She wasn't thinking about the legality of the situation. She only wanted him to stay.

Carrie swallowed hard at the memory of it. She forced herself to think of something else. Namely, what she would say to him when she saw him. Her impulse would be to fling herself into his arms but being impulsive in the past had taught her many hard lessons. She'd never heard from him after he left, so it was obvious he had forgotten her. She'd simply been a means to an end.

Biting her lip, she pulled the inflight magazine from the pocket of the seat in front of her and decided to do some duty-free shopping. It was time to push Mick Foley out of her mind, just as he had pushed her out of his life.

She managed to doze awhile on the overnight flight and woke to the announcement of the impending arrival into Shannon. Carrie leaned against the window to try and get a better view of the west of Ireland as the plane made its descent. But heavy cloud cover prevented her from seeing anything.

Once they landed, she met with Kathy and, following the rest of the crowd, they wound their way through corridors and up and down escalators until they came to Customs. There were only two officials manning desks and one line was for those people who were EU passport holders. Carrie and Kathy stood in the other line behind the rest of the Americans and Canadians.

After they cleared customs, it was a short walk to collect their luggage from the carousel. With their suitcases trailing behind them, they made their way outside to the curb to flag down a cab.

"I don't know about you, but I feel like we lost a night's sleep there," Carrie said. They'd left at nine the night before and it was now nine in the morning. The flight had only been six hours.

Kathy giggled. "I hear you. I feel punchy."

"So this is jet lag," Carrie mused, wondering if she could somehow squeeze in an afternoon nap. Anywhere.

The taxi driver threw their luggage into the trunk of his car and climbed back into the front seat.

"Where to?" he asked.

Carrie pulled out a slip of paper from her purse and rattled off an address in Kilcornan.

The cab driver, a man with a shaved head, nodded and smiled. He looked back at them and asked, "Are you here for the festival?"

"We're here as impartial observers," Carrie quipped.

The cab driver chuckled. "Of course you are."

"I already have a boyfriend," Kathy piped in. "Although if I get a better offer, I'd have to seriously consider it."

The cab driver looked at Carrie, but she shrugged, holding her palms up. He studied them both for a minute, and Carrie wondered whether he was assessing them to see if they'd be able to land themselves a man at the festival, or whether he was divining her fate. He sighed and turned around. His pronouncement was not encouraging. He began to head east, toward the middle of the country.

Kathy folded her arms and looked out the window. "I know David. He'll read my note and think, 'Ah, she'll be home in a few days once she pulls herself together.' And when he gets home from work, he'll sit on the sofa and eat pizza and drink beer."

Carrie nudged her friend and smiled. "Come on, don't get yourself worked up. Forget it for now and you can work it out when you get home."

"I don't know if I want to." Kathy turned to her, and her eyes glistened with tears. "I thought he was the one. I thought he loved me. But here we are, three years later, and we are going nowhere. It probably hasn't even occurred to him to ask me to marry him," she humphed.

"I know you're upset, but try to have some fun while you're here," Carrie encouraged.

Kathy nodded and forced a smile.

Tired from jet lag, the two of them stared out the windows at the passing scenery. Carrie was impressed at how green everything was. She hadn't known a lot about the country. She had no Irish ancestry in her English, German, and Polish genes. She knew people back home took their Irish heritage very seriously, and of course St. Patrick's Day was a very big celebration, but other than that, she had never paid much attention to the little island. But she had to admit to a certain curiosity about catching up with Mick and finding out how he ended up as a matchmaker. That was as far removed as possible from his college degree. His degree had been in history, and she recalled that he'd wanted to be a high-school history teacher. An old-fashioned matchmaker—a role traditionally filled by women. There had to be a great backstory there.

She'd googled Ireland and learned a few basics: it was a country of almost five million people, there were some pockets of the country where Irish was still spoken, and Dublin was the capital. Despite the conflict of interest, she'd decided to do her best. She could hardly beg off the assignment; then she'd have to tell her boss that the matchmaker was her husband. And that would be a story of its own.

She leaned against the window, and her eyelids felt like they weighed a ton. With her eyes focused on the green outside, she soon fell asleep.

The cab driver gave a loud rap on the ceiling of his taxi, startling Carrie awake. She stretched and looked over at Kathy, who had also fallen asleep. They paid the driver, got themselves and their luggage out of the car, and stood in front of their hotel. Carrie looked around the town and took everything in.

The main road was narrow and winding, flanked on both sides by terraced houses that had been converted to shops. They were painted in bright shades of yellow, blue, red, green, and orange. The road barely allowed for two cars to pass each other comfortably. There were roadblocks set up to pedestrianize the area for the festival. The road ascended toward a stone church at the top of the town. In the opposite direction, shops and buildings petered out and from her vantage point, she spied a leafy park.

Despite being a small village, she could now see there was a certain buzz about the place. Bunting of red and white triangular flags crossed from one side of the street to the other. Shop windows were lined with red and white fairy lights.

"Are we going to stand outside all day or are we going to check in?" Kathy asked with a nod toward their hotel.

The Caherdavin Arms was a three-story structure that was painted white. Window boxes on the upstairs windows held the beginnings of spring shoots. A sign above the door read,

"Caherdavin Arms." To the left of the black enameled front door hung a brass bell and a brass letterbox.

Carrie pushed through the front door and found herself inside a spacious foyer with a black-and-white diamond-tiled floor. A luxurious wallpaper with a peacock pattern covered the walls. There was a brass umbrella stand with no umbrellas in it and a large stone hearth with a blazing fire. A sofa sat perpendicular to the fireplace, facing a pair of leather club chairs. At the centre of the arrangement, a black Labrador lay sound asleep on an ottoman in front of the fire. He did not lift his head when they walked in.

"This is so cozy," Carrie said, looking around.

"It's beautiful," Kathy agreed.

Carrie looked up at the high ceiling with its ornate plasterwork. A wide, carpeted staircase wound around to the upper floors, its dark banister gleaming in the light.

They looked around and found no one, but there was a bell with a plastic placard next to it that read, "Ring for service."

Carrie rang the bell, and still the dog didn't move. She wondered if she should check for a pulse. Within minutes, they heard hurried footsteps, and a middle-aged woman with a blonde coif appeared.

"Welcome to the Caherdavin Arms!" she said, extending her hand. She spoke in the lilting way of the Irish, but Carrie detected an American accent. "I'm Sarah Caherdavin."

Carrie and Kathy shook hands with the woman. "I'm Carrie Fields and this is my friend, Kathy McClintock. We've booked a room."

"Of course," the woman said. She was polished: hair a beautiful shade of blonde that didn't occur in nature at that age, eyes a piercing blue, and lips painted a flattering shade of matte red. Her clothes were upper retail and her perfume smelled expensive.

"We've got you on the third floor. Unfortunately, the elevator is broken, but there's a man coming tomorrow to fix it." She grimaced. "Is that going to be a problem? I'd move you to another room but with the festival, we're booked solid, as is every other hotel and B and B in town."

"No, we can manage until tomorrow, can't we Kathy?" Carrie looked at her friend, who nodded. Carrie asked the woman, "Is that an American accent I hear?"

Sarah laughed. "Guilty. I'm originally from Ohio. But I came here twenty years ago to check out the festival with my friend, and I never left. Met my husband on the first night. We decided to open up this place. And the rest, as they say, is history!"

"That's so romantic," Kathy practically cooed.

Carrie eyed her friend. She wasn't getting any romance in her life right now, and it made her vulnerable to sappy stories. But Carrie herself held firm.

"Are you here looking for love?" Sarah asked.

Carrie immediately shook her head. "Oh no, I'm here to interview the matchmaker."

Sarah frowned. "Mick? Really? I'm surprised. He's such a private person."

Carrie wondered about her words as Sarah turned to Kathy and said, "And what about you? Are you hopeful for love? Romance?"

Kathy shook her head faster than Carrie had.

Sarah laughed and raised her eyebrows. "We'll see. When love is in the air here, it's highly contagious."

Carrie and Kathy looked at her, doubtful, but said nothing.

Once Sarah got some help to carry their luggage, she led them up the old, creaking staircase to the third floor.

"With the elevator out, it certainly keeps me fit, running up and down the stairs," Sarah said with a laugh.

"Do you like living in Ireland?" Kathy asked.

Sarah looked over her shoulder at them. "Oh, I love it! I was a corporate girl back home, in the rat race. The lifestyle here is so laid back, and the Irish people are just lovely."

"And is your husband involved with the running of the hotel?" Carrie asked.

A shadow passed over Sarah's face. "No, unfortunately, he was killed ten years ago."

"That's awful. What happened?" Carrie asked. Kathy gave her a slight elbow as if to say, *Mind your own business.*

Sarah sighed. "Roger was an avid cyclist. He was hit by a lorry and killed instantly."

Carrie and Kathy stood there with their mouths wide open, staring at Sarah in disbelief. Kathy spoke up. "We're so sorry to hear that. But it's wonderful that you stayed here at the hotel."

Sarah shrugged. "When it first happened, I seriously thought of taking our daughter back to the US. But we had invested so much time, money, and effort into the place that it would have been a shame to leave. Plus, our daughter, Amy, was in the primary school and had friends. The people of Kilcornan were wonderful to me, and I just loved the town too much to leave."

Carrie had seen the town; it didn't seem like there was much to love.

After Sarah showed them to their room, she departed.

Their standard room housed two double beds. It was wall-papered in fleurs de lis and had high ceilings. The window offered a great view of the main street. Because she'd had the short nap in the taxi, Carrie figured she might as well stay up and try to make it to bedtime.

Carrie and Kathy chose their beds and unpacked their suitcases.

"You know, there's no reason you shouldn't partake in all these matchmaking festivities while we're here," Kathy said as she hung up some blouses on the rail on the inside of the door.

Carrie shrugged. "I'll hardly have time for that. I've got to interview the matchmaker as well as some couples who met at the festival."

"I know you've had some bad experiences on dates, but not all men are jerks," Kathy pointed out.

Carrie snorted. "You mean all those blind dates from hell?" She fell back on her favorite reply: "When the time is right, I'll meet the man of my dreams."

Kathy gave her a tight smile. "You're going to have to be a little more proactive than that."

Carrie had never told her that she'd married Mick all those years ago. She hadn't told anyone. Not even her parents or any family or friends. Looking back, she could see it had been an impulsive, reckless move of youth. She'd never bothered tracking him down for a divorce, because she'd always been hopeful that he'd come back to her.

Beginning to feel depressed, Carrie changed the subject. "Will we go and explore the town?"

Kathy frowned. "You know, I have a wicked headache, so I might just lie down for a bit."

Carrie nodded. Kathy's phone chirped; she picked it up and grimaced. "Ha! A text from Lance Romance," she scoffed, referring to David. "Get this: no 'Hello, where are you?' but, 'When are you coming home?' He must be out of clean socks.

Oh well!" She threw the phone on the bed and went into the bathroom.

"I'm heading out!" Carrie called after her.

"All right, Carrie," said Kathy. "See you in a bit."

Carrie stepped out of the hotel and surveyed the main street. She wondered about meeting Mick after all these years. She thought of the various ways she could play it. Her first thought was to be casual, as if their short marriage had meant nothing to her. Or she could be witty and chatty, to show him what he'd missed. In the end, she decided she'd just be professional. But then there was the horrifying thought that he wouldn't remember her at all. That didn't bear thinking about.

Carrie blew out a hard breath and tried to still her beating heart. People milled about in the street. Speakers located throughout the town center played love songs. Elvis crooned a mournful ballad as she stepped up to gaze at the spring colors and florals in the window display of a dress shop. She looked down at her own business casual and thought maybe a dress might be in order.

As she debated whether or not to go in and browse through the racks, she happened to look up.

That's when she saw him.

An audible gasp escaped her lips.

All those years that had come and gone since he'd left, now evaporated. She was nineteen again and shy and trying to navigate adulthood.

But she'd know him anywhere. He stood sideways to her, his hands on his hips. With nostalgia, she remembered that little quirk of his. He wasn't alone; he was with a couple, and their conversation appeared animated. He had filled out and was even more solid than she remembered. The mop of hair was now worn short. Carrie stood rooted to the spot. Her heart thumped hard and she tried to still her pulse. All sorts of feelings came at her as she watched him. Feelings she'd never had for anyone else but him.

It was hard to believe that he fixed people up for a living. He was as unlikely a matchmaker as there could be.

He began to turn in her direction. Alarmed, Carrie put her head down, pulled her purse close to her, and slipped into the shop. *Maybe I will go dress shopping after all,* she thought.

The one thing she knew was that when she reunited with Mick Foley, she planned on having the upper hand.

CHAPTER FOUR

MICK SAT IN HIS small office in a side room off his sister's café. He took a cursory glance at his appointment calendar. Now that the festival was in full swing, he was booked solid. Both men and women sought him out to find the love of their lives. Mick would do his best, as always.

"Hi, Mick!" boomed a voice.

Startled, Mick looked up to see Charlotte Connors standing in the doorway. He had to suppress a groan. He remained seated to avoid any hugging, which Charlotte was quite fond of. She looked the same as she always looked: wearing big, thick glasses, a skirt that went down to her ankles, and a cardigan that had embroidered flowers on it. She reminded him of a grandmother, yet she couldn't be forty.

Charlotte Connors ran a blog from Cork City about dating and whatnot. She was a regular fixture at the matchmaking festival. This had to be her third or fourth year in attendance.

She'd done a profile of Mick and the festival on her blog years ago. And when she found out that the matchmaker himself was single, she'd more or less made it her mission to find him a mate. Specifically, herself.

"How are you, Charlotte?" he asked politely.

"I'm well, thank you for asking," she said. "Although I have to admit to being disappointed that you haven't taken me up on my offer to show you Cork in all its glory."

Mick shrugged. Charlotte invited him every year to come down to Cork City and avail of her hospitality, which included a stay at her home. Mick had no intention of going to Cork to stay with her. It was bad enough that she tried to hang on him for the duration of the festival. He avoided answering her question by asking one. "How long are you in town for?"

Charlotte grinned. "I'll be here for the whole two weeks!"

Mick resigned himself to his fate and stood up from his chair. "It's good to see you again, Charlotte, but I have to get back to work." He paused and added, "These people won't get matched up themselves."

Charlotte laughed. A little too long and a little too hard. She also made no move to leave. "I'd love to help you with that. We'd make a great pair," she gushed.

When he said nothing, she asked, "Would you like to grab some dinner tonight?"

"Charlotte, that's probably not a good idea. I like you as a friend, nothing more," he said firmly. Then to soften the blow, he added, "Besides, I've got to work late anyway."

"How about after work? Maybe we could get a drink," Charlotte pressed, ignoring what he'd said.

Mick shook his head. "I don't drink."

"Oh, that's right," she said, her voice trailing off as she ran out of ideas and invitations.

Charlotte was a nice person. And Mick knew beyond a shadow of a doubt that somewhere in the world there was a man for her. But that man wasn't him.

"I'll see you around then?" he asked.

She smiled and said, "Yeah, sure. I'm staying at the Emerald Isle B and B."

Mick nodded but said nothing either way.

Silence fell between them and finally, Charlotte mumbled, "I'll see you later, Mick." And was gone.

Mick breathed a sigh of relief. It was going to be a long two weeks. He'd just turned his back to the door when he heard a rap on the doorframe. Thinking it was Charlotte returning for round two, he rolled his eyes and sighed before turning around.

"What—"

But it wasn't Charlotte.

Her looks were leonine. Strawberry-blonde hair around a heart-shaped face and amber-colored eyes. A fitted cobalt-blue dress hugged her curves and just skimmed her knees. But it was the eyes. He'd know those eyes anywhere. He'd never forgotten them.

Mick's mouth fell open and he blinked several times in rapid succession. His voice shaking, he said, "Carrie?"

"Hello, Mick," Carrie said.

"Carrie!" He said again, not quite believing his eyes. He hadn't seen her in years and yet she'd managed to find him. He broke into a wide grin. "How did you find me?"

He thought briefly about taking her in his embrace, but Carrie crossed her arms over her chest and looked away.

Mick ran the gamut of emotions. He'd always hated the way he'd left things with her. She'd helped him out by marrying him and he'd ended up abandoning her.

"I work for the *Philly Chronicle*," she explained.

"You always wanted to be a journalist." He smiled.

"You remembered," she said softly.

He'd remembered a lot about Carrie Fields. *Carrie Foley*. They'd gotten married and although they'd only been together for three weeks, he'd never forgotten her.

She hated coffee but she loved tea. She had a tendency to be clumsy. She played a lot of card games.

"What brings you here to Ireland?" he asked, shoving his hands into his pockets. It was so good to see her after all this time. It was like the sun coming out after a long spell of rain.

"I'm here for work," she explained. "One of our reporters was supposed to interview you. Barbara Edson? But she's taken ill and our editor has sent me in her place."

Mick rode off the roller-coaster high of delight to the stomach-dropping feeling of disappointment.

Carrie hadn't sought him out. It was a work assignment that had brought her here. Not him. He swallowed a lump in his throat that he suspected was his pride.

"Where are you staying?" he asked.

"The Caherdavin Arms," she replied.

Mick nodded. "Great place. Sarah is a lovely person."

"Yes, she is," Carrie agreed.

"Are you here alone?" He couldn't help but wonder if she had a significant other. Being married had certainly held him back, and he wondered if it had done the same for her.

"I'm here with my friend Kathy," she said.

Carrie was not a beauty in the usual sense, but to him, she was breathtaking. She had what was called "presence." That was the only way he could describe her. And he'd been captivated by her when he first met her all those years ago in the bar up on the Cape. She'd been so different from the other girls that came in and flirted with him, who were loud and obnoxious at times.

"Can I get you a cup of tea?" He then asked quickly, "You still drink tea, don't you?"

She nodded with a smile. "I do, but I'll have to pass. I just wanted to touch base about the interview for the newspaper."

"Of course," he said too quickly.

"Do you have a minute?" she asked.

"Yeah, sure," he said.

"I'd planned on covering three parts in the feature," she started. Using her fingers, she ticked them off one at a time. "The history of the festival and the matchmaking, something personal about you, and what the future holds for traditional matchmaking in the era of online dating."

This was Mick's busy time of year, but he would make time for Carrie. He really wanted to catch up with her.

"Also, Barbara had hoped to interview a few couples that were set up by you?" she asked.

Mick nodded. "Sure. I had three couples in mind. One was set up by my grandmother, one by my mother, and one by myself. Is that all right?"

"Yes, that's perfect."

He drank in the sight of her, deciding he was going to draw this out so he could spend time with her. Whether she wanted to spend time with him or not.

"Come in and sit down," he invited.

Carrie looked around the small office and finally settled into a chair.

Mick looked at his calendar and glanced over it. He was booked solid, but he'd fit her in somewhere. As they hammered out details of an arranged appointment, Mick realized a few things about Carrie. First, her perfume was lovely, something light and floral and not overpowering. And she was still shy. She'd been so quiet and shy when he'd met her. But now there was something else—aloofness? Guardedness? He felt like she was keeping him at arm's length. It wasn't at all the happy reunion he'd always dreamed about. But what did he expect? He'd left her all those years ago with not so much as a backward glance.

Her appearance had changed. When he'd known her all those years ago in Cape Cod, she wore glasses, her hair in a ponytail, and was always seen in college sweatshirts and jeans. But now, she looked more put together. Professional. Back then, when he first leaned over the bar to talk to her, he had quickly discovered that there was a fierce intelligence behind those glasses.

He listened attentively as she spoke about the feature and how she was tweaking it to put her own stamp on it. She bent her head and scribbled something on the notepad. Mick noticed her hands were trembling.

"Carrie, how have you been?" he asked, searching her face. Her face, which had been so animated when she discussed the article, immediately shut down. She appeared wary.

What had he done? He lowered his gaze, unable to meet hers.

"I'm fine," she said. "I've been with the *Chronicle* since I left college."

"Are you happy there?" he asked, lifting his head.

She nodded quickly. "Very. I'm doing what I love."

"Good." Mick let out a huge breath he hadn't realized he was holding.

Carrie folded the notebook closed and stood up. Mick jumped up from his chair.

She looked up to him and said, "Look, no one knows about us. I mean, what we did all those years ago. I would appreciate it if you wouldn't mention it to Kathy."

"Of course," he said immediately.

She backed up, bumping into the chair and losing her balance. Mick reached out for her, but she'd grabbed onto the chair and steadied herself.

"Still clumsy as you can see," she said with a nervous laugh. Mick smiled.

"See you around, Mick," she said and disappeared out the door.

Once she was gone, Mick stared at nothing for a long time.

Rosemary appeared in the doorway with her hands on her hips. "What's this I hear you've canceled all your appointments for the afternoon?" she demanded.

Mick looked away from the blank wall he'd been staring at. "Huh?"

"You're not working! What's wrong?" she asked.

Rosemary and Mick were cut from the same cloth. There was purpose in work and routine, and they rarely deviated. They were happy creatures of habit. They weren't the types to get sick and they rarely went on vacations. Rosemary didn't like flying, and Mick didn't like traveling alone. So, they stayed put. And worked. As their parents had done before them.

"What happened? Is it that Charlotte again? Has she finally pushed you over the edge?" Rosemary said.

Mick shook his head. "No, it's not Charlotte at all," he said, his voice trailing off. How could he tell his sister about Carrie and what he'd done to her all those years ago? How he'd married her and then left her?

He got up from his chair and brushed past his sister. "I need some fresh air."

"Mick—" Rosemary called out after him, but he kept walking. "What about your appointments?"

He didn't answer her. He thrust his hands in his pockets, picked up his pace and headed out the door in the direction of the top of the town. His chest tightened and breathing became difficult. He drew in some big gulps of air and forced himself to calm down.

In his quest for immediate solitude, so he could think, he walked past the shops and a straggle of festivalgoers, not even stopping to chat or give them a quick wave in salute.

He walked past the church to the graveyard behind it. He strolled through the cemetery, landing at the family plot. He read the names of his parents and grandparents on the plot that had been used by the family for generations. Up here on the top of the hill behind the church, you wouldn't know there was a festival going on down below. The only sounds were a few bumblebees buzzing around the purple and yellow wildflowers that grew along the edge of the cemetery, and the distant whine of a lawnmower.

He stood at his mother's grave, looking at the headstone, almost hoping she could somehow provide some of her much-missed wisdom. But no answers were forthcoming.

Looking around and seeing no one there, he muttered under his breath.

The selflessness of Carrie's offer to marry him so he could stay in the US had made a deep impression on him. Especially since she was the sole reason he didn't want to go home.

On a rainy day at the end of August, they'd gotten married in a civil ceremony in Boston with two strangers acting as their witnesses.

For Mick, it had been the happiest day of his life.

CHAPTER FIVE

CARRIE STOOD AT THE window of her room later that evening with her arms crossed over her chest, watching the activity on the street below. Three stories up, she had a bird's-eye view. What amazed her was the throngs of people that had descended on the little village of Kilcornan. Despite the chilly weather, men and women of all ages milled about on the streets. She watched as some of them came out of one dance hall and carried on to the next pavilion.

Due to jet lag, it had been an early night, although Kathy's phone had blown up with texts from David to the point where she had to turn it off so they could get some sleep. Apparently, he had no idea of the time difference.

Carrie had gone to bed still reeling from her earlier encounter with Mick. More than once, Kathy had asked if she was all right. Was she? She didn't know.

As Kathy snored lightly on the other side of the room, Carrie reviewed her reunion with Mick. He had appeared surprised, and that had given her a sense of advantage. But the feeling had only lasted about ten seconds. What she hadn't expected—and should have anticipated—was the tidal wave of emotions that rolled over her on seeing him after such a long time, making her feel once again like a shy teenager with a heartbreaking crush on a guy.

He looked great, which didn't surprise her, but his reaction to her had. He seemed genuinely happy to see her, and that made her more confused than ever. She'd expected ambivalence, or worse, indifference. After all, he'd made no attempt to get in touch with her these last ten years. But instead, he seemed genuinely happy.

A deluge of memories of their wedding day overwhelmed her. For her, it had been a day so full of promise. Admittedly, she had had her own agenda in marrying Mick. She'd been sporting a supersized crush on him and had hoped he would grow to love her once he got to know her. In hindsight, she realized she might have been delusional.

She'd traded in her jeans and sweatshirts for a vintage 1960s knee-length dress with long sleeves and a lace overlay. She'd even had her hair done. She left her glasses at home and had to constantly remind herself not to squint. Mick had sheepishly handed her a small bouquet of daisies for the occasion, mumbling, "Every bride deserves flowers." She'd been rendered speechless by the gesture.

They had just three weeks together after the ceremony. She'd told no one what they had done. Not her family. Not Kathy. Not her friends. Besides, they were all back home in Philadelphia. But those few weeks had been whirlwind. Mick had suggested they 'hang out' together. And they did.

She taught him how to play poker and all sorts of card games. He took her to museums in Boston and introduced her to Irish music, giving her a CD of Irish music to play in her car.

It had been the happiest time of her life. But early one morning, her phone rang. It was Mick. He was on his way to the airport, he explained. His mother had passed away unexpectedly. He had to go home. She was understanding.

The last thing he'd said to her was "I'll come back."

Carrie never saw him again.

"Are you still awake?" Kathy asked, her voice groggy.

"Too excited about being here," Carrie lied, climbing back into bed and pulling the covers over her.

"Go to sleep or you'll be dragging tomorrow," Kathy advised in the middle of a yawn before rolling over onto her other side.

Despite being exhausted from jet lag and lack of sleep, Carrie woke with the pearly gray light of dawn. She could see someone below in the street, kicking something along the pavement.

She turned her thoughts to her job and the story she was supposed to write. If there was one thing Carrie knew, it was that work was a great distraction from worry. She jumped out of bed and headed for the shower, a plan for her story beginning to take shape.

"While you were working on your notes this morning, I made some inquiries in town about this festival and the matchmaker services," Kathy said to Carrie.

The two of them sat next to each other on a tour bus. They were heading up to County Meath for a guided tour of Newgrange. Carrie wanted to get a feel for the place and the country. So far, she had been impressed by the scenery: golden valleys, green hills, herds of livestock, and narrow country roads.

Carrie raised one eyebrow but said nothing, deciding to let her friend prattle on.

"I met with the matchmaker—he's not too shabby," Kathy said in an approving voice. Her dark hair framed her face.

Carrie's eyes widened in alarm. "Why? Why would you do that?"

"Because you need to find someone. At the very least you need to go on a date," Kathy explained.

"No, no, no," Carrie protested. "I'll be too busy working."

"Never mind that, you'll have time to meet some eligible men. You're on vacation!"

"*You're* on vacation. I'm on assignment," Carrie countered.

"It won't hurt for you to go out with a few guys while we're here, just to have some fun," Kathy said as the bus lurched dangerously along a narrow road. "Who knows, maybe some nice Irish guy will sweep you off your feet."

Carrie didn't know how to tell her that a nice Irish guy had already swept her off her feet a long time ago.

"I had a talk with Mick Foley about you," Kathy said.

Carrie blanched and felt the contents of her stomach begin to make the return trip.

"I told him you were a wonderful person who deserved to find someone special," Kathy said.

"You did what?" Carrie cried in panic. She leaned forward in her bus seat, resting her head against the back of the seat in front of her. "Why would you do that?"

"Because enough is enough. Enough with the dismal blind dates."

"What did he say?" Carrie asked. She didn't want Mick to think she was actively seeking a partner. That was not the message she'd wanted to send.

"He said he'd have no trouble finding us matches. That it should be no problem."

Carrie cringed. Despite her good intentions, Kathy had just made things more awkward than they already were between her and Mick. And what about Mick? Was he so eager to foist his wife on someone else? She was both appalled and angered. She leaned back in her seat and stared at the ceiling.

"The majority of the people who come to this festival are single," Kathy said.

"Obviously," Carrie said. "It is a matchmaking festival after all."

Kathy nodded. "Did you know there's a wall in the café that's covered with photos of happy couples of all ages and nationalities?" She sighed and added, "At least there are some happy couples out there."

Carrie gave her best friend a reassuring smile, glad to be on the safer topic of Kathy's own love life. "I know you're hurting over David, but I'm here for you."

Kathy laughed. "Thanks, Carrie. This will do us both a world of good, you'll see."

"I thought you and David were only taking a break," Carrie pointed out.

"We are, and I made that very clear to Mick Foley. That I wasn't interested in a match per se, just looking for some masculine company while I'm in town."

"Good, is that what you told him about me as well?" Carrie asked, hopeful. She didn't want Mick to think she was looking for a new husband. They weren't even divorced!

"No, of course not! I told him you were a free agent, that there was no one back home and you were the adventurous type," Kathy said.

Carrie groaned. She didn't want Mick to think she was some kind of lonesome loser back home. That she hadn't carried on after he'd left. Meanwhile, he'd probably had loads of girlfriends since he'd returned home. Why had she taken this assignment? Why hadn't she become a teacher as her mother told her?

Carrie pretended to have a keen interest in the scenery outside the window. It was beautiful to be sure; everything was so green. The low stone walls gave the landscape a honeycomb effect.

"He certainly is thorough, that's for sure. Asked all sorts of questions about you."

"Like what?" Carrie asked.

"Have you had a lot of boyfriends, have you ever been in a serious relationship, what were your views on marriage . . ."

"What business is it of his?" Carrie asked, annoyed.

"He's just doing his job. I mean, how can he fix us up if he doesn't know anything about us?"

"What did you tell him?" Carrie asked with a grimace.

Kathy laughed. "I told him that although you weren't seriously involved with anyone, you were the queen of disastrous blind dates!" Once she stopped laughing, she sighed. "I wonder if he's married. He certainly is hot."

Carrie frowned. "You think he's hot?" Carrie couldn't deny it; she thought he was hot, too. In a primitive, jungle-drum kind of way.

Kathy grinned. "Oh, yeah. Tall, dark, and handsome!"

"I may just tweak this a bit," Carrie mused out loud, feeling conflicted. On the one hand, she didn't want Mick to think she was available but then, on the other hand, she was still smarting over his leaving her all those years ago. It irritated her that her love for him had been one-sided. Maybe she should play it cool:

be aloof with him and have a good time and show him what he'd missed.

"There's no tweaking needed," Kathy warned. "This isn't going to be like the tenth grade, is it? When I wanted to leave Josh Parker a note in his locker, but you said leaving a note on his porch at home would be better, and I ended up with a dog bite on my bum?"

"No, of course not," Carrie said, dismissing her with a wave of the hand.

"You decide to 'tweak' a perfectly good idea or 'fix' things, and it always sounds good but then trouble happens."

"Okay, other than you getting bit by the dog, what else has gone wrong?" Carrie asked, slightly annoyed.

Kathy looked at her. "Really? You're really going to ask me that?"

"Nothing is coming to mind," Carrie said.

"Let me refresh your memory," Kathy started.

Carrie grimaced; her friend had a memory like an elephant.

"Does 'I found a budget tour of Mexico' ring any bells?" Kathy asked. "When I wanted to go on a cruise?"

Carrie conceded with a shrug. "Okay, so that wasn't a good value."

"Wasn't a good value? I ended up with Montezuma's revenge and had to go on IV hydration when we got home!" Kathy said.

"All right, all right, if that's it . . ." Carrie said, trying to head her friend off at the pass.

"Oh wait, I'm just warming up," Kathy said. "How about that double date?"

Carrie frowned, pretending not to understand.

"Oh no you don't—you remember that. You needed me to go out with you and Jason Siegel because his cousin was in town. Nice guy, you said. Kind, he said. It was like being out with an octopus! I never knew where his hands were, and he seemed to have more than two.”

Carrie cut her off because she sensed Kathy was on a roll. “All right, but this is different.”Kathy’s eyes widened. “How? How can this possibly not end up with me getting pawed, bit, sick, or anything else?”

“First, we’re only here for two weeks. And second, I’m only tweaking it on my behalf.”

Kathy sighed and looked out the window. “Carrie, you make it sound so easy, and yet something invariably goes wrong.”

By the time they arrived back in Kilcornan, it was late afternoon. They enjoyed Newgrange, but Carrie’s claustrophobia prevented her from going inside the tomb’s chamber. She had started in, but as soon as she felt the walls of the tomb pressing against her shoulders, her breathing became ragged and she backed out, almost knocking down the elderly lady behind her. Shaking, she mumbled an apology and dashed for the open air.

The dog was sound asleep on the ottoman in front of the fire.

Carrie looked over at him. “Do you think he’s dead? I mean, he hasn’t moved since we arrived yesterday. Has he had his dinner? Used the bathroom? Does he need anything?”

“Why don’t you go ask him?” Kathy asked with a laugh.

Sarah Caherdavin appeared in the lobby.

“Is the dog all right?” Carrie asked, frowning with concern over his motionless figure.

Sarah followed her line of sight. “Arthur? He’s fine. Why?”

"Because I haven't seen him move since we got here," Carrie said.

Sarah laughed. "Arthur is thirteen years old and hardly moves anymore. That's his favorite spot, and sleeping is his favorite activity."

Carrie wasn't convinced. "Does he bite?"

"No, that would involve too much energy."

Satisfied, Carrie turned away from the dog and asked, "What can you tell us about the resident matchmaker?"

Sarah shrugged. "Mick? He's good at what he does. He has a gift for matching people up with the right partner. It's uncanny really."

"Did he fix you and your husband up?" Kathy asked.

Sarah shook her head. "No, his mother did. And the funny thing is, my husband isn't someone I would have picked for myself."

"Really?" Kathy asked.

Sarah smiled at the recollection. "When Mrs. Foley first matched us up, I complained to her that Roger wasn't my usual type. And she said, 'Maybe your usual type hasn't worked in the past.'" A dreamlike quality shadowed her face. "And you know, she was right."

"So Mick learned the trade from his mother, then?" Carrie asked.

"I suppose so. I know he says the same thing she used to say, that Irish men and American women are a great match but not vice versa."

Carrie noted this in her brain for later use in the article. "Does he have a girlfriend?"

Sarah shook her head. "That's the sad part about it. I can't ever remember him with a serious girlfriend. He's dated, but it never seems to work out."

"That seems odd, that he can find matches for other people but not for himself," Kathy suggested.

Sarah shrugged. "I can't explain it. But there's nothing the people of this town would love more than for Mick and Rosemary to find their true loves."

"Who's Rosemary?" Carrie asked.

"His sister. She owns the café," Sarah explained.

"Why do the townspeople care so much whether they have partners or not?" Kathy asked with a frown.

"The Foleys are such a lovely family. Their mother was a remarkable woman. They're always helping everyone. Anyway, we'd just like to see them happy."

"Maybe they already are. There's nothing wrong with choosing to be single," Carrie said.

"Of course not, but this town is all about love and romance," Sarah reminded her.

Carrie said to Sarah, "Kathy has the bright idea that we need to avail ourselves of the matchmaker's services."

Sarah smiled. "Be prepared to be surprised."

Chapter Six

MICK WAS AT HIS desk in his office the following evening. He usually loved that it looked out over the street and the café, as he liked to watch people. But he was expecting Carrie and her friend, and he found he couldn't focus on anything. His sister popped her head into the room.

"Mick, your next appointment is here, a couple of very pretty Americans," Rosemary said with a grin.

He nodded, nervously wiping his hands on his pant legs.

When Kathy had been in to see him the previous day, he'd bristled internally at the idea of fixing them up with a couple of fellas for the length of the festival. Carrie was, after all, a married woman. He didn't like the thought of her going out with someone else. But he reminded himself that when he'd left her, he'd given up any right to exclusivity. He couldn't expect a woman like Carrie to be faithful to a marriage that had been in name only. That would be unfair to her. Still, not for the first time, he wondered why she'd never located him for a divorce. Maybe she had no plans to remarry. His thoughts were interrupted by the arrival of Carrie and Kathy.

He stood up quickly, knocked his chair on wheels astray, and quickly righted it. "Come in and sit down."

Kathy immediately sat in the chair closest to him. Carrie looked at everything in the room except him.

But Mick spoke to Carrie first. "Breda and John Horan will stop by your hotel tomorrow morning for an interview. Hope that's all right."

She finally looked at him and nodded. "That's fine. Thanks."

"I understand you ladies are looking for me to match you up," he started.

Carrie lifted her chin a slight bit. "I don't need any help in getting 'matched up.'"

"Don't be spiky," Kathy whispered.

"I'm just saying," Carrie said.

Mick immediately tried to put her at ease. "I'm sure you don't need any help finding a date back home"—here Carrie shot him a look— "but while you're here in Ireland, I can find you some suitable company, nothing serious of course, as Kathy has stated."

"What if I wanted something a little more serious?" Carrie shot back, her eyes narrowing.

"Then I'd be more than willing to help you find a mate," he said. He didn't remember her being this antagonistic when they were together. Had he remembered it wrong? Gold-plated their time together?

He nodded and took two clipboards off his desk. There was already a questionnaire and pen attached to each one.

"If you don't mind, you can fill these forms out and look over the packages and pricing below," he said.

Carrie eyed the form from top to bottom and her eyebrows lifted.

"Wow, you're pricey!" she said.

Kathy elbowed her and gave her glare. "Don't worry, Carrie, this is my treat."

"Do you always say what you feel?" he asked. Years ago, she'd been so shy. She must have found her voice. Good for her, he thought.

"She does," Kathy piped in. "She can't help herself. She doesn't have a filter for her mouth."

Kathy carried on speaking directly to Mick. "Carrie's always about her career. Hardly ever goes out, no serious relationships. One dating disaster after another."

"Is that so?" Mick asked, amused, leaning back in his chair and putting his hands behind his head.

"You don't have to give him a play-by-play of my life," Carrie hissed to Kathy.

"Details are good," Mick said, enjoying himself. It was clear that Carrie didn't want to be there but her friend had other ideas. "Dating disasters, did you say?"

"Oh yeah," Kathy said, warming up to the subject. "Carrie's got that market cornered. Let's see. There was the blind date with Will."

"Don't, Kathy, please," Carrie said, reddening.

"Carrie met Will online. They went on one date—" Kathy stopped because she had started laughing.

"What happened?"

Kathy couldn't stop laughing so Carrie explained. "Will failed to mention that he was eighty-two. To this day I don't know if he was looking for a girlfriend or a carer."

"Then there was Johnny," Kathy said, still laughing.

Carrie groaned. "At the end of the first date—a lovely meal at a restaurant—he asked me to lend him some money. I thought he meant for the tip. But he was looking for five thousand dollars!"

Kathy picked up the thread of the conversation. "And don't forget about Paul."

Carrie looked at Mick and then said, "He's not interested in hearing all of this."

"I am, really," Mick said truthfully. And he was. He wanted to know what Carrie had been up to since he left.

"Look, we won't take up any more of your time," Carrie said, all businesslike. She took the pen off the clipboard and scanned the form.

"What kind of questions are these, anyway? 'What's your favorite color?' Really? 'Do you like to cook? Or eat out? What are your views on climate change?' And, 'There's only room for five people in the boat but there are eight of you, who's going overboard?'"

She looked at him with something close to revulsion on her face. Amused, Mick grinned. "It's an ancient family formula that we use," he teased with a tap to his temple.

Mick never gave any of the questionnaires a glance, it just seemed to him that if people were handing over hard-earned money, they should at least have a chance to fill out a comprehensive form, beyond the vital statistics and information. How could he explain to Carrie and Kathy, or anyone for that matter, that fixing people up was an intuitive, sixth sense? That was one of the reasons he avoided interviews. He'd be laughed out of the country if he put his skills down to some New Age bull. He didn't understand it himself, but his mother had taught him long ago that it was a gift, not to question it too much and to just go with it. It was advice that he never forgot.

He studied their bent heads while they filled out their forms. Kathy filled hers out quickly, while Carrie seemed to agonize over some of her answers. He wondered if she was seriously looking for someone. A sense of relief had filled him at the fact that there was no one serious waiting for her back home. And although Kathy did have someone back home, she'd made it clear to Mick earlier that she was not interested in a relationship. Just looking for someone to go dancing and hang out with. He appreciated her honesty. Over the years, he'd dealt with a lot of chancers.

Once they finished filling out their questionnaires, they handed the clipboards back to him. He set them down on his desk and stood up. "Okay, let's go," he said.

"Wait, aren't you going to read what we wrote?" Carrie cried.

"Oh, sure," he said. He picked up both clipboards and went right past what they'd written, down to the bottom of the form. "All right, Kathy, you're interested in meeting two prospective guys and Carrie, who's more ambitious, is interested in meeting five." He looked up and saw her blush. "Is that correct?" he asked her.

She swallowed hard. "Yes. But aren't you going to read our answers? So you can pick someone appropriate?"

"Yeah, sure. I'll study them later," he said. He had no intention of looking at them later.

"Good," Carrie said. "I don't want to be fixed up with just anybody."

"Noted."

"But you're just going to introduce us to someone right now?" she protested. "Don't you have research to do?"

Mick frowned. "Trust the process, ladies. Come on, let's go." As they walked out of the café, Mick thought long and hard. He had to be very careful with Carrie. He wanted to fix her up with someone who wouldn't hassle her but at the same time, he didn't want her to find the guy attractive. This was going to be tricky.

"Did you want some form of payment in advance?" Kathy asked.

"You can just drop the cash off tomorrow," he said. "Ready?"

He headed down the street with the two of them alongside him. People greeted him and waved to him, calling out his name.

"Have you lived here all your life?" Kathy asked.

"Yes, my family has been here for generations," he answered.

"Other than your sister, do you have family here?" Kathy asked.

"No, my parents are dead."

Carrie glanced at him but looked away.

"I thought you were the interviewer," Mick said with a laugh.

"I'm saving my questions for the interview," Carrie said drily.

As they walked along the road, the O'Donovan sisters approached.

"Mick! Yoo hoo!" called Maeve.

Despite the sunny days, the April air still had a bit of a nip to it, and the two elderly women had dressed accordingly in blouses, tweed skirts, cardigans, and sensible shoes.

"How are you feeling?" Mick asked Millie. "Maeve said you were under the weather."

Millie gave a dismissive wave with a gnarled hand. "I'm fine. One shot of whiskey and I was as good as new."

Mick introduced Carrie and Kathy to Maeve and Millie.

"Are you availing of our favorite matchmaker's services?" Millie asked.

"We are," Kathy said.

"It's hard to believe that you two would need the services of a matchmaker. You're both so pretty. Don't you think so, Maeve?" Millie said.

Maeve nodded. "They wouldn't be the first Americans to find themselves Irish husbands, now will they, Millie?"

"No, that's for sure." Millie regarded Mick, then looked at both women and back to him. "Now if we could just find a nice girl for our Mick!"

Mick laughed. "Millie, I'm just waiting for you to say yes. A man can only take so many refusals."

Both the ladies giggled like schoolgirls.

Maeve eyed Carrie thoughtfully and said to Mick, "You know, you two might make a good match. I like the look of the two of you together."

Millie picked up on the idea. "Oh, yes. She's blonde, he's dark. She's short, he's tall," she crowed, clapping her hands.

"Are ye trying to steal my job right from under me?" Mick teased them, trying to get them off the subject. He noticed Carrie had said nothing, just blushed. "Will ye join us at the pub for a pint?"

Maeve shook her head. "No, too many people, don't want to end up with a broken hip. We'll head home and have our whiskey with our tea."

"Ladies, I won't keep you."

"Maybe you'll meet the love of your life tonight, Mick," Millie sang.

"Maybe the cow will jump over the moon," Mick replied.

Again, both women laughed and waved him off. "Ah, go on!"

Mick led Carrie and Kathy into a pub called Dirty Bertie's, known for always managing to snag a good band, and currently packed with sweaty revelers.

"Wow, it's busy in here," Kathy said nervously.

"Is the festival like this every year?" Carrie asked, her eyes widening as she looked around. She bit her lip.

"Yes," he answered honestly.

"That's kind of sad," she reflected.

"How do you mean?" he asked.

"All these people looking for love?" She practically winced, as if the thought of it made her too uncomfortable.

Mick regarded her for a moment and said softly, "And yet here you are, looking for love yourself."

Her cheeks reddened and she avoided his gaze.

He clapped his hands and she jumped. "Okay, let's find some dates for you ladies," he said. "And don't forget, we've got all sorts of couples' activities that take place during the festival. I'm the organizer, so just let me know if you want to participate." He looked around. "Wait here. I'll be right back."

As he walked, he scanned the faces in the crowd. He kept in mind his agenda to keep Carrie busy but not too interested. His goal was to keep her occupied until he figured out what to do with her. There would be no problem finding either girl a mate or a date or whatever they were looking for. Both were pretty, as the O'Donovan sisters had said.

But Carrie had an indefinable spark about her that he rarely came across. She had that luxurious mane of strawberry-blonde hair with golden highlights, but it was her amber eyes that gave her an exotic look. When she had stood next to him, barely reaching his shoulder, the urge to protect her had nearly overwhelmed him.

As he made his way to the back of the pub, he glanced around, looking for suitable candidates for Carrie and Kathy. He took a deep breath in and let it out slowly, opening himself to the possibilities that might arise.

In the corner was a fella from Waterford, not bad looking, but Mick immediately dismissed him. He was known for telling crude jokes.

Then he spotted Martin against the back wall, watching the action on the small dance floor as tight-packed couples swirled around. Martin was a nice man but incredibly shy, and Mick worried that the girls' personalities might be too much for him. He was still on the lookout for someone special for Martin, but the man needed to be handled with care.

There was Leonard walking through the crowd, slightly hunched, but hopeful. But he still lived with his mother and had some strange ways.

He eyed two fellas in the back corner talking over a pint, who were regulars at the annual festival. Amazing, how they never managed to meet anyone permanent. Their friendship had developed when they met here years ago. Ronan was a farmer over in Carlow who was a confirmed bachelor and came down for the fun, and Eddie worked in an auto parts store over in Kildare.

Suddenly a vision of Kathy with Ronan came to mind, and Mick felt like it would be a good fit, albeit a temporary one. He didn't want to picture Carrie with anyone.

"Hey, Mick, what's the craic?" Eddie asked.

Mick gave them both a nod of acknowledgment.

"Fellas, would you be interested in meeting a couple of American women? Nothing serious. They're just looking for some fun." Thinking of Carrie, he added quickly. "They're looking for a couple of gentlemen."

Ronan, tall and languid and leaning against the back wall, immediately stood up straighter.

"Follow me," Mick said, and headed back to the Americans.

Chapter Seven

"Is he coming back?" Kathy asked with a nervous laugh. "Do you see him?"

Carrie looked for Mick. He was taller than most of the people there, but the crowd of the pub had swallowed him up. She was beginning to doubt her plan. Quietly, she fumed. She'd planned to play it aloof and get matched up with a few men. She just didn't think Mick would go along with it with so much enthusiasm.

"Maybe this isn't such a good idea," Kathy said, biting her lip and echoing Carrie's thoughts. They spied Mick heading in their direction with two men in tow. "Oh look, here he comes now." Kathy smoothed her hair with her hands. Carrie folded her arms across her chest.

"That was fast! Are we that typical and unchallenging?" Carrie wondered out loud. She bristled at the thought that he found her predictable. He hadn't even seen her in ten years, and he thought he could find her a match in five minutes? The thought rankled her.

Carrie tried to get a peek at the men, but Mick's large frame was blocking them from view. She hoped there wasn't a man looking like a twelve-year-old behind him.

"Ladies, I'd like to introduce you to some fellas," Mick said. He stepped aside to reveal two men with eager looks on their faces. One was tall and dark-haired with amazing blue eyes. Next to Carrie, Kathy cleared her throat.

The other guy was about five-ten and solid, with tattoos snaking up his arm. He had a wannabe bad-boy vibe going on, but it was falling short of the mark. It might have been his lazy eye.

"Kathy, this is Ronan," Mick said, introducing Kathy to the tall, dark-haired guy.

"Hi," Ronan said shyly, extending his hand. "Nice to meet you."

Kathy hesitated and Carrie had to nudge her to shake the man's hand. Carrie resisted the urge to roll her eyes. This had been Kathy's idea, after all.

Carrie could feel the other man's eyes on her. He gazed at her like he'd just won the lottery.

"And Carrie, this here is Eddie," Mick said. Mick continued to grin, and Carrie couldn't help but wonder if he was making fun of her. This possibility infuriated her.

"Can we buy you ladies a cocktail?" Eddie asked.

Carrie looked over to Kathy who shrugged and said, "Sure, why not?"

"I'll leave you to it," Mick said with a smile, and wandered off. Carrie's eyes followed him until he was no longer in sight. She couldn't help but wonder what he was doing next. And who he was doing it with.

"Well, what'll ye have?" Ronan asked.

"How about a margarita or a piña colada?" Kathy suggested brightly.

Eddie laughed. "I'm afraid you won't get that here."

Kathy's smile disappeared. "Okay. Maybe a martini."

Now Ronan laughed. "Try again."

Carrie interrupted. "Why don't you tell us what they do serve?" She didn't want to stand there all night, with sweaty bodies pressing up against them from all sides, trying to guess.

"The usual: ales, stouts, beers, wine, spirits like whiskey, vodka, and gin," Eddie put forward.

"That's great," Carrie said, trying to sound agreeable. "We'll both have a Guinness."

"Great," Eddie said, and then he leaned in to Carrie and whispered, "Stay right here, I'll be right back."

Ronan gave Kathy a gentle smile and the two men headed off to the bar in search of beverages.

"That Ronan seems sweet," Kathy said, her eyes never leaving the form of the tall farmer.

"He's very handsome," Carrie offered.

"Hmm, he sure is," Kathy agreed.

"Not too sure about my guy," Carrie said. She was beginning to wonder about the matchmaking skills of Mick Foley.

"Why not? He seems nice," Kathy protested with a slight hesitation in her voice.

Nice wasn't the word that came to mind for Carrie. It was going to be a long night. But then she thought that might work in her favor. She could make the best of it and then report back to Mick that they were great dates. She could also grill both men about their take on the goings-on of the festival for her article.

Once they reappeared with the drinks, Carrie asked, "Is this your first time at the festival?"

Eddie smirked. "No, we've been coming here for five or six years now"

Kathy laughed. "Five or six years! And you haven't found someone yet?" she cried in disbelief.

Ronan took a step back and then shuffled his feet. "We don't come here looking for brides," he said. His tone sounded defensive.

Immediately, Kathy put out her hand, laid it on his arm and said gently, "I'm sorry, that wasn't a nice thing for me to say. I know how hard it is out there, trying to find someone."

Ronan nodded at Kathy with a smile, the slight forgotten.

"What about you, Eddie?" Carrie asked. "No luck yourself?" Surely there was someone out there for him. Especially if he'd been coming there for years.

"Nah, but I come more for the *craic* than anything else," he said.

Carrie blinked. "Crack? You come for the crack cocaine?" What kind of village was this? Suddenly, a story started forming at the back of her mind. Matchmaking festival front for drug running and possibly money laundering? Reporting crime had made her suspicious.

Eddie and Ronan burst out laughing.

"*Craic*," Eddie said, spelling out the word for them. "It's an Irish word for good time or entertainment."

Kathy laughed with relief. "Oh! You had us worried for a minute."

Disappointed, Carrie sipped her drink and took a brief look around the room. Her eyes caught Mick's at the other end of the pub.

Her heart rate picked up. Again. Even after all these years, he still had that effect on her.

Their eyes held steady for a moment, until he lifted his glass to her in a salute and Carrie forced herself to look away. She purposefully turned her attention back to Kathy, Eddie, and Ronan.

"What about ye?" Ronan asked. "Any boyfriends back home we need to worry about?"

Carrie looked over at Kathy and wondered how she was going to answer that one. Kathy was someone who was pretty upfront.

"I do have a boyfriend back home," Kathy said, and she stared at her pint glass.

Ronan blanched and Eddie raised an eyebrow.

Kathy sipped her drink and continued. "But we're taking a break, and I'm just looking to have some fun."

"He won't show up here, will he?" Ronan asked nervously.

Kathy laughed. "Not on your life. I couldn't get him to take me out to dinner and a show, so I know he won't travel three thousand miles to see me."

Carrie detected a mixture of sadness and disappointment in her friend's voice, and she wanted to strangle David for being so obtuse. He'd never find anyone better than Kathy. And Kathy'd always been crazy about David. Carrie remembered when Kathy first met him and how she gushed about him being "the one." She shook her head. Maybe relationships were just not worth the trouble.

Eddie was talking about something, and Carrie feigned interest. Casually, she sipped her drink and looked over to where she'd last seen Mick, but he was no longer there.

John and Breda Horan, the elderly couple Mick had suggested Carrie meet with, appeared at the hotel right on schedule the next morning. Breda had a curved spine and John used a walker to get around.

Sarah had graciously allowed Carrie to use the conservatory room at the back of the Caherdavin Arms, a glass-walled room that was bright with sunlight. Carrie had to move around a bit to find just the right chair for herself and the Horans so the sun wasn't shining in their eyes.

"How long have you been married?" Carrie asked after introductions were complete and the Horans were settled with a cup of tea.

John and Breda looked at each other, almost as if they were unsure. "What's it about? Fifty-five years?" Breda asked.

"That sounds about right," John concurred.

"And you met at the festival?" Carrie asked.

John nodded.

"What made each of you decide to come to the festival to seek out love?" she asked.

"It was my girlfriend's idea," Breda said. "I was just going with her so she wouldn't have to go alone. I had no intention of meeting anyone at the festival."

"Why not?" Carrie asked.

"Because I'd just become a qualified nurse," Breda said. "I had plans to go to England to work."

"And you, Mr. Horan?"

"Well, I was a little more hopeful than Breda. That year was my fifth year attending. Now, in the past, I'd had a good time.

The *craic* was good, as they say, but I hadn't met anyone special until I met Breda."

"And tell me how you met," Carrie prompted.

The couple looked at each other and smiled.

"I got hit in the head with a flying object," John said with a laugh. "A beer bottle!"

Carrie winced.

"And I saw it happen and went to see if he was all right," Breda explained.

John's face softened at the memory. "She was so caring. She led me out to a seating area, and I sat down and she looked me over—"

"He was so handsome. He had a headful of black hair," Breda interrupted with a smile. "And he had a nice goose egg on his forehead!"

"At the time, I said to myself, 'I'm going to marry that girl,'" John said with a dreamy expression on his face, reliving the moment.

"How did you know?" Carrie asked.

John shrugged and looked at Breda. "I couldn't tell you how, I just knew that I had met my future wife."

Carrie didn't say anything, but that was how she'd felt when she met Mick. Never before or since had a man made such an impression on her.

"We sat there in the front of the hotel and drank tea, and we talked for three hours. I felt like I'd known him my whole life. Do you know what I mean?" Breda said.

Carrie nodded, knowing all too well. She and Mick could talk and talk, and it had always felt to her as if she'd known him her whole life.

"You never made it to England?" she asked, looking up from her notebook.

John spoke up. "We went to England right after we got married. Breda worked as a nurse, and I worked as an electrician."

"But we returned to Ireland after five years," Breda added.

"Once the children started coming." John smiled. "To be nearer to our families."

Breda turned to John. "Do you remember that first night we met, when we were sitting in the lobby talking to each other, there was a cat? A beautiful black cat with white paws. He looked like he had socks on," Breda said. "He slept on the edge of the sofa the entire time we were there. Do you remember the cat, John?"

"I do remember the cat." John nodded, leaning forward on his walker. He had a faraway look in his eyes. "That cat is long gone, but by God, we're still here."

"We sure are." Breda laughed.

Carrie found herself sighing. This feature was turning into a nice distraction from writing about crime all the time. After her interview with the Horans was over, she thanked them and walked them to the front door.

Chapter Eight

M ICK WAS UP EARLY, still thinking of Carrie. She was due in at ten for the first part of their interview. He was anxious to see her and anxious not to see her.

Mick didn't know why he'd hung around the pub last night when he should have just gone home and either picked up his book or finished his crossword puzzle. But he'd wanted to keep an eye on Carrie and make sure she was all right. That's what he told himself. He was surprised at his disappointment when he saw the two women with Ronan and Eddie, laughing and appearing to be enjoying each other's company. He'd frowned, bought himself a Coke at the bar, and settled in against the front wall of the pub to observe the goings-on—the shenanigans, as his mother used to call them.

He'd tried not to stare at Carrie, but it was just about impossible not to. She had the most gorgeous hair he'd ever seen. Not for the first time, he wondered what it would feel like to run his fingers through it, or even just to touch it. Her face was animated and her eyes big and bright as she relayed some story to Eddie. What could she be telling them? He watched as Ronan and Eddie burst out laughing and he couldn't help but feel jealous, wishing it was him that she was talking to and laughing with. But he knew he had no one to blame but himself for the current state of affairs: him standing alone and Carrie in the company of another man.

When he had married Carrie, he'd never told her the reason he'd wanted to stay on in the US was because of her. He wanted to get to know her better. He had a terrible crush on her. She was so different from any other girl he'd ever met.

And spending time with her had only reinforced his feelings for her. Cemented them. And only days before he'd left, he'd planned on telling her that he was falling in love with her. He'd also bought her a ring: a simple gold band. They were married and he felt she deserved a ring. The weather had been beautiful in September of that year. They'd planned a picnic in the park in downtown Boston that day. They had been having a great time and getting along really well. And he was pretty confident that she felt the same about him that he had felt for her.

But his plans had been spoiled by an early morning phone call. His mother was dead. She'd been found dead in her bed that morning by his sister. Mick had been stunned into silence and numbness, the picnic and the ring in his front pocket, forgotten.

The last thing he'd said to Carrie before he hung up the phone was, "I'll be back."

But he never did go back.

Carrie was punctual. She said good morning and took the chair Mick offered but refused his offer of tea.

As she settled herself in by hanging her purse off the back of her chair, opening her notebook and uncapping her pen, she seemed to be avoiding looking at him.

"Did you enjoy yourself last night?" he asked.

She nodded but didn't smile. "It was a lot of fun. My feet hurt from dancing."

"I'm glad it worked out," he said.

"We're seeing them again tonight," she announced.

Mick raised his eyebrows. "That's great." He tried not to sound too encouraging.

"Shall we get started?" she asked, glancing at the clock on the wall.

"Sure." Mick nodded. "Will we talk about the history today?"

Carrie looked up from her notebook. "Yeah, that would be great. I'd like to talk about your family matchmaking business and the history of the festival."

"Are you sure you won't have a cup of tea?" he asked.

"No thank you," she said. "I just had breakfast. Tell me how a matchmaking festival got started here in Kilcornan."

"It was not uncommon in Ireland years ago, more than one hundred years ago, for there to be matchmakers. Farmers were busy tending their livestock and fields and had no time to look for a bride."

Carrie listened intently and jotted down notes from time to time.

"But each year, in September, after the harvest was over and the farmer was flush with cash, he might meet with a matchmaker to find him a wife."

"Is that what your family did?" Carrie asked, looking up from her notebook.

"Yes, my mother's family have been Kilcornan's match-makers for as long as anyone can remember. My great-grand-mother was legendary, with a great level of success. They came from all over Ireland to see her. That's how the festival evolved. There were so many people coming to see her that it turned into a great big festival in September at the end of the harvest."

"So it wasn't always in April, then." Carrie said.

"In the beginning, no, but as the years went on and the clientele wasn't so predominantly farmers, it was changed. It was actually my mother who thought it would be a good way to jump-start tourism in the area, by having the festival for two weeks in April."

"Obviously it appears to have been successful."

Mick nodded and smiled. "You know what they say about spring and a young man's fancy."

Carrie gave him a small smile and asked her next question. She continued her interview for the better part of an hour, focusing on her work.

Mick liked the way her hair hung like a drape, framing her face as she bent her head to write down some notes.

They were startled by a loud rap on the doorframe.

"Mick, I've been looking all over for you," said Charlotte.

Mick scowled at the intrusion. Charlotte wore a jean dress with ladybugs embroidered all over it, and on her legs were black-and-yellow striped tights. Even her way of dress was loud.

Charlotte gestured toward Carrie. "I didn't know you had company."

Mick regarded her evenly. "Yes, I do, so I'll talk to you later."

Carrie jumped up from her chair. "That's all right. I'm finished for now, Mick."

Mick stood up after her. "There's no need to run off. Let's finish this." He was aware that Charlotte was taking in the whole interaction between them.

"Another time," Carrie said. She gave Charlotte a quick smile and disappeared out the door.

"What did she want?" Charlotte asked.

"I fixed her up last night with a match," Mick answered indirectly. He didn't want to tell Charlotte that he'd agreed to an interview. He'd never hear the end of it, and she'd bug him until kingdom come for the same.

"Gee, can't she find anyone in her own country?" Charlotte asked sourly.

"She's a reporter from the *Philadelphia Chronicle* and is doing a story on the festival. Probably wanted to kill two birds with one stone."

"Oh, Mick, you're so funny," Charlotte said with a laugh.

Mick said nothing more, hoping Charlotte would take the hint and walk away.

"Hey, not to change the subject, but I see Kilcornan's newspaper is for sale," Charlotte said.

Mick studied her and said nothing. He was afraid to give her any ideas. It was bad enough that she came here for the two weeks of the festival. The last thing Mick wanted was for her to live here.

"I've grown to love Kilcornan just like my own town," Charlotte said, as if reading his mind.

If Charlotte moved to Kilcornan, he didn't think he could stand it.

"Wouldn't that be something?" Charlotte said, scratching the back of her head.

"Wouldn't it just?" Mick agreed. "I've got to get back to work." And he left her there and headed out.

There was a sharp chill to the air that evening. After reading the same paragraph over and over again, Mick finally put his book down and picked up his crossword puzzle. But he was stumped on a nine-letter word meaning "to dupe or deceive." Eventually, he gave up and went for a walk to clear his head. Being with Carrie in person again had left him muddled and unsettled. The feelings he'd had for her had remained with him; he realized that they had never left.

But the question was what to do about all of that.

As he walked on, the shouts and laughter of the revelers and the music became more muted. Sometimes, he just needed some quiet to think. The village transformed from blocks of terraced houses and shops into detached dwellings with substantial front gardens and driveways. If he kept walking, he'd get past the single houses and end up on farmland, where it was one pasture or field after another. But it was getting dark out, and he turned and headed back into town.

He strolled back toward home. He was in no hurry, and he walked with his hands in his pockets. He liked getting a feel for the festival. And this year's one was off to a good start. He was just coming upon the pub when the door opened and the music spilled out. Carrie and Kathy with Eddie and Ronan emerged from the lively pub.

Mick could hear snippets of their conversation. Ronan wanted to take the girls dancing, but Eddie wanted to go to the chipper. Mick hung back as he didn't want Carrie to see him. He didn't want it to look like he was following her. Suddenly it seemed to him that she was everywhere. Everywhere, that is, except with him.

As Mick lived in the flat above the café, he made it his last stop of the evening before heading upstairs, just to say hello to people. The café would be open for a while yet, having extended their closing for the duration of the festival to midnight. Rosemary had gone home to take a break for an hour and left the café in the capable hands of two of her employees. The place was mobbed with people enjoying a cup of tea and a sweet.

Mick was surprised to bump into Dennis, the produce man. He almost didn't recognize him coming in through the front door and not wearing his uniform. Dennis was dressed casually. He kept brushing back his short hair with his hand.

"Hey, Dennis," Mick saluted. "What brings you out?"

Dennis's eyes darted around. "I think I may have left something here from my delivery. I was just going to ask Rosemary."

"Rosemary's gone home. But come on, I'll see if I can find it."

Dennis bit his lip. "Huh, I thought Rosemary was working late."

"She is, but she went home for a break and is coming back later."

Dennis sighed. "Right, then. Catch you later, Mick," he said. He turned on his heel and walked away.

Mick called out after him, "Don't you want to look for—"

"Never mind, I just remembered I've got to do something," Dennis said, and he disappeared down the street.

Mick smiled after him. Rosemary had an admirer. It was about time.

As he made his way through the café, an arm from a booth reached out and tugged at his sleeve. He turned and found a woman of about forty giving him a sheepish smile. On the table in front of her were a half-finished cup of tea and a half-eaten scone. Sitting across from her, a man about the same age propped his head up with his hand, his elbow resting on the table. Mick could tell he'd had way too much to drink.

"I'm sorry to bother you," the woman started. "My name is Marie. I wanted to tell you about our story."

Mick stopped in front of the table. This was the best part of his job; people always approached him and wanted to share their stories.

"Oh, not this again," groaned the man in the booth with her.

The woman glanced at the man and appeared to hesitate.

"Tell me," Mick prompted gently.

"I came here ten years ago to the festival. I actually had an appointment with you, but I met Jim before then and so there was no need to keep the appointment. We have three children."

The woman beamed.

But the man cut in. "Pay no attention to her; she's a pain in the neck."

Marie's mouth opened slightly, and the joy that had softened her face disappeared. She looked at Mick apologetically and gave him a small smile.

Mick looked at the husband. "You're a lucky man."

He was sorry Marie hadn't kept her appointment with him; he would have found her a much more suitable match. Or at least someone who felt the same way about her as she did about him.

To save Marie any further embarrassment, Mick said good-night and walked away. He couldn't help but think of his own unsuccessful marriage. And he concluded that maybe love wasn't for everyone.

CHAPTER NINE

C ARRIE STOOD AT THE bar waiting for the round of drinks she'd ordered when the woman who'd interrupted her meeting in Mick's office elbowed her way in next to her. Carrie glanced at her briefly and looked away, noting her interesting choice of clothing and accessories. The woman pushed her big glasses higher on the bridge of her nose.

"I heard through the grapevine that you're a reporter," she said.

Carrie did a double-take. "Are you talking to me?"

Charlotte nodded, sipping her drink from a tumbler, the ice cubes clinking against one another. She handed Carrie a business card, and Carrie squinted to read it in the dim light: "Charlotte Connors, blogger, Cork City."

"Carrie Fields, *Philly Chronicle*," Carrie said.

"I heard you're here to do a story about the festival."

"I am," Carrie replied. "Well, more of a feature on Mick Foley, with some highlights about the festival."

"You're interviewing Mick?" the woman asked, her drink halting midway to her mouth.

Carrie nodded.

"That's odd, because Mick Foley doesn't usually grant interviews," Charlotte said, taking a sip of her drink.

Carrie shrugged with a smile. "I don't know what to tell you. The arrangements were in place before I took the assignment."

"Have you finished interviewing him?" Charlotte asked.

Carrie shook her head. "I've just started."

"I'd be willing to talk to you about him."

"Why?" Carrie asked, confused.

Charlotte glanced around. "I've been coming here to the festival for years. And, well, Mick and I . . ." she said with a smirk. "You know."

Carrie didn't know, and she certainly didn't want to assume anything. Charlotte didn't strike her as Mick's type, but then what did she really know about what Mick's type was? It had been clear that whatever it was, she wasn't it.

"Are the two of you . . . involved?" Carrie said.

"Not yet." Charlotte smiled. "But we're heading in that direction."

Carrie wanted to tell her not to hold her breath.

"What do you want from me?" Carrie asked, sounding more abrupt than she intended. The news that Mick was in some kind of relationship had upset her.

Charlotte spoke. "I thought we could throw our lots in together. I can tell you what I know about Mick, and you can provide me with some details for my blog."

Carrie paid the bartender and picked up the drinks. "Thanks, but no thanks. I don't need any help, and anything you want to know about Mick you should probably ask him yourself." She stepped away, trying not to bump into anyone or let the drinks slosh over the sides of the glasses. She shook her head, thinking about what a strange woman Charlotte was. She wanted nothing to do with Mick's new love interest. She certainly didn't want to swap stories or compare notes.

For the rest of the evening, Carrie and Kathy spent their time in the company of Ronan and Eddie. Kathy seemed to have taken a shine to Ronan. And although no sparks flew with Eddie, Carrie had to admit that he was a fairly decent dancer.

Ronan mentioned that he was there for the full two weeks, and Carrie studied Kathy's reaction. Her friend, still fresh from her "break" from her long-term boyfriend, began to suggest things she and Ronan might do together. Carrie tried not to be alarmed, but she was worried about Kathy. And about herself. If Kathy was going to be seeing the sights with Ronan, Eddie might get ideas about spending time alone with her. But fate came to the rescue as Eddie announced he'd be leaving in a few days to head home and go back to work. Thank goodness. She needed to work on her article. She supposed it might be nice for Kathy to have someone to share outings with.

During the dancing and the traveling back and forth between the dance halls and pubs, Carrie kept her eyes open for Mick. She told herself it was all in the name of the article she needed to be writing. It had nothing to do with the fact that every time she saw him, her heart did a little backflip while her stomach somersaulted. It bothered her that she was still attracted to him after all this time. She had to keep reminding herself that he had left her. Without looking back.

After a few hours, the four of them left the pub, and at Eddie's suggestion, they headed to the chipper for some fast food. Carrie walked next to Eddie, and Kathy and Ronan followed behind them.

"Oh great, here comes the garda." Eddie snorted derisively.

Carrie looked up to see a man approaching them. By his uniform, she pegged him as a cop. He wore a yellow hi-vis jacket over a short-sleeved shirt, and navy-colored pants.

"Well, well, who do we have here?" The garda laughed as his eyes locked with Eddie's.

"Calm down," Eddie said. "We're just heading to the chipper for some grub."

"But it's never just one thing with you, is it, Eddie?" the officer asked.

"We've got dates for the evening, and we're going for a bite to eat," Eddie said forcefully.

The garda glanced at Carrie and Kathy and said, "The generosity of women never ceases to amaze me."

Carrie laughed, but Eddie rolled his eyes.

"Ladies, I'm Paul Nash, and if you're in any kind of trouble"—he looked pointedly at Eddie—"or if you think trouble is about to happen, I'm here." And he walked on.

"What was that all about?" Carrie whispered to Eddie.

Eddie shrugged and muttered, "Just a past misunderstanding."

Carrie couldn't help but wonder if that misunderstanding had led to a court conviction and jail time. What kind of man had Mick set her up with?

The chipper was an establishment located at the end of the street, between the only bank in town and a dress shop. Carrie's stomach growled as they walked through the door. She narrowed her eyes against the bright illumination of the takeaway, a small place with no tables. A big overhead board displayed the menu, with pictures of the choices on offer.

The place was crammed with people. In the corner, Carrie spotted Mick. He was deep in conversation with two men, and the conversation must have been good because their laughter was loud. Mick looked up suddenly, locked eyes with her, and smiled. The hair prickled on the back of Carrie's neck, and she looked away, embarrassed.

"Earth to Carrie, hello in there," Eddie called.

Carrie snapped her head around. "Oh, yes, what?"

Eddie laughed. "I asked what you would like to eat?"

Carrie looked at the board quickly and said, "I'll try those taco chips."

Eddie frowned. "Is that it? Do you want a burger or some chicken?"

Carrie shook her head. "No, thank you, the chips will be plenty."

He laughed again. "You're easy." His gaze lingered.

Carrie's eyes widened and she thought, *No, I'm not!* "I'll wait outside. It's too crowded in here."

She stepped outside, glad for the fresh air and space. The crowds of people that had filled the streets, the pubs, and the dance halls all day were beginning to thin out as it neared midnight. The pubs in Kilcornan closed at half twelve. She watched a couple strolling down the street arm in arm. She leaned against the wall of the takeaway, yawning and wondering if they had just met or had been together a long time. She figured the former, because there was an excited air emanating off them.

She didn't notice or hear the door to the takeaway open until Mick stood beside her.

"How is it going with Eddie?" he asked.

She looked up at him, wondering if he was making fun of her. She regarded him evenly and decided that two could play at that game.

"It's going. He seems nice," she said. She refused to give him any satisfaction.

"What do you think of our little town so far?" he asked.

"From what I've seen, I like it. The festival sure is a lot of fun," she remarked. They had shifted positions so they wouldn't have to look at each other. Whether that was a conscious, concerted effort on their parts, Carrie didn't know. They stood shoulder to shoulder, looking out at the street.

Carrie glanced over, liking the way his bicep tugged against his shirt. He smelled of some spicy aftershave that made her want to sigh.

"Can I ask why you don't like to give interviews?" she ventured. Her motto was: the answer is always no unless you ask.

He looked down at her and shrugged. "I just don't. I'm a very private person."

"Hmm, I see. Do you own and operate the café as well?" she asked.

"No, that's my sister's business. I own the building and have my office there."

"What is your percentage of success with matching people up?" she said.

"I don't know, I never analyzed it."

Carrie doubted this; he seemed like a man who knew all the details. Backward and forward.

"I think people should find their own mates. Intervention is never a good idea. Neither is help from well-meaning friends," Carrie observed. Relaxing, she leaned back against the wall.

He grinned. "Are you speaking from personal experience?"

"Not particularly," she muttered.

A small crowd of people walked by in the middle of the street, their arms around each other, singing. A few them called out to Mick. A group of young women ran past, laughing and shouting, "Hi, Mick!"

He waved to them and laughed. "Mind yourselves now."

Carrie watched as the group walked away. "You know a lot of people."

"It's a small town, and we do get a lot of regulars for the festival."

"If there are so many regulars, then the matchmaking must not be one hundred percent foolproof," she said, eyeing him. She pivoted away from the wall and faced him, her arms folded across her chest. The night air was chilly.

"Nothing ever is," he said.

A silence descended between them like a heavy cloud.

Mick spoke first. "I was just looking to catch up, so why don't we save the interview questions for our meeting tomorrow morning," he said, his expression serious and his eyes intense. Carrie found she couldn't look away.

"Tough to catch up on ten years in five minutes," she said, wishing she had bitten her tongue. She did not want him to think she was bitter.

"I'm sorry to have bothered you. Goodnight, Miss America," he said quietly, and stepped away.

That startled Carrie. That's what he used to call her when they first met. She rubbed her arms briskly, trying to shake off the feeling.

She watched as he walked away, head down, hands in his pockets. She'd thought she was making conversation. She didn't think she was interviewing him. He soon disappeared, and Carrie decided he had trust issues.

Carrie was in her bed but hadn't yet fallen asleep when Kathy came back. Her friend closed the door softly and tiptoed through the room.

"I'm awake," Carrie said in the dark. Thoughts of Mick had made sleep elusive.

"Oh," was the response, and then, "Can I turn on the light?"

"Yeah, sure," Carrie said, sitting up in her bed. "What time is it?"

"Almost two," Kathy said. The light went on, and Carrie closed her eyes momentarily against the brightness.

"Have you been with Ronan all this time?" Carrie asked, wondering if her best friend knew what she was doing.

Kathy flopped onto her bed, lying back with her feet still on the floor. "I am so tired."

"Where were you?" Carrie prodded gently.

Kathy sat up. Her face looked relaxed. "After you and Eddie left, Ronan and I walked to the end of town. There's an old stone bridge there, and we just sat for an hour and talked."

"Gee, it's kind of cold out," Carrie said. "And dark."

"The moon is very bright tonight." Kathy smiled. "Not too cold. It was nice. And he was attentive and kind."

"What about David?" Carrie asked. Kathy was in a vulnerable position; she technically was on a break from her boyfriend, but they still lived together.

"Ugh!" Kathy said, rolling her eyes. "He's been texting me all day long. If only he had paid this much attention to me when we were together, then I wouldn't be here, sitting on a bridge in the middle of the night with a stranger."

"What does David want?" Carrie asked.

"The usual. When am I coming home, come home so we can talk. And then there was my favorite: what did I do with his hockey stick." Kathy bounced up and shook her head. "I'm wrecked. I'm going to wash my face and brush my teeth, and then I'm going to bed. What's on the agenda for tomorrow?"

Carrie yawned. "I have to work, so I'm afraid you're on your own. You don't mind, do you?"

Kathy shook her head. "Of course not. I might do something with Ronan. He said he wants to show me something."

Carrie burst out laughing. "Oh, I bet he does!"

Kathy giggled. "Not anything like that. He knows about David. We're just spending our time together while we're here at the festival, that's all."

"All right, but just be careful. I don't want to see you get hurt," Carrie said.

Kathy laughed, picked up her nightgown, and headed off to the bathroom. "All right, Mom."

Carrie was up early the following morning, as soon as the dawn broke. She walked softly around the room so as not to wake Kathy, who appeared to be in a deep sleep. After she showered, she dressed quickly and put on minimal makeup. She left a note for Kathy telling her she'd see her later and exited the room, closing the door softly behind her.

The town was deserted; aside from the decorations, you would never know that there was a festival going on. Carrie loved this part of the morning, anywhere in the world, when the sun was rising and everyone was still asleep. The whole day was still ahead of you and full of hope. An early morning riser by nature, she liked to plan her day out with a good cup of tea. But this early in the morning, nothing appeared to be open. All the shops were shrouded in darkness. But there were lights on in the café, so Carrie made her way there.

Chapter Ten

Mick had opened the door to the café early in the morning as he was expecting Carrie. He'd asked her to come before his appointments and before the café opened for the day so they'd have time to carry out the interview uninterrupted.

"Good morning, Miss America. Right on time," he greeted her.

"Could I trouble you for some tea? The gas station wasn't open yet."

"I'll make us a pot." He jumped to his feet. He added with a grin, "Why would you want to drink petrol-station tea?"

"I didn't want to be a bother," Carrie admitted.

"It's not any trouble," he said. He walked past her and closed his eyes briefly when he got a whiff of her perfume. He balled his fists at his sides.

"All right then," she said.

"Do you still drink it with one sugar and a splash of milk?" he asked, stepping behind the counter.

A slow smile emerged on her face. "You remember."

He shrugged. "I didn't forget."

Mick put the kettle on and pulled a white china mug from the dish rack. "Did you sleep well?"

"I did. You?"

"Like a baby," he said, pulling down a canister of tea bags from the shelf.

The conversation, though polite, was stilted.

"I've always been an early riser," Carrie said. She had her purse slung over her shoulder and her arms crossed over her chest.

"I remember that about you," he said with a smile. "Always eager to conquer the day."

"Not much has changed since you left," she said. He didn't know whether that was a shot across the bow or what.

"I see nothing is open in town yet," she commented.

The kettle boiled and Mick rinsed out a stainless-steel teapot with the boiling water before filling it again and throwing in a couple of tea bags.

"Nothing this early," he agreed. "Most shops don't open until ten. The café opens at nine and the grocery store opens at eight."

"What are you doing up so early?" she asked.

He looked up from what he was doing, and his eyes locked on her amber ones. She was still mesmerizing. How could he have walked away from her? He knew the answer to that. Grief.

"I'm always up this early. This is the best part of the day," he said.

"I agree."

From the industrial-sized refrigerator, he took out a small white porcelain jug of milk. Once he fixed her tea, he slid the cup across the counter to her.

"Just like old times," she said softly.

"Yeah, just like old times," he agreed.

"Thanks," she said.

"What would you like with it? A scone? Some toast and marmalade?"

"A scone would be nice," she said. "If it's not too much trouble."

"I think I can handle putting a scone onto a plate," he said with a laugh.

Once she had her scone, she looked around the café.

"Grab a table," he said. He watched her out of the corner of his eye as he wiped down the counter. A flurry of ideas filled Mick's mind as to what could be done to make things right with her. For what he had done all those years ago.

Mick stepped out from behind the counter with a cup of tea in his hand and joined Carrie at her table. She'd set her purse down on the floor and sat with her legs crossed at the knee. And they were a fine set of legs, he thought: shapely, with narrow ankles. She buttered her scone and spread a bit of strawberry jam on it.

Mick set his cup of tea on the table. He took the chair next to her, flipped it around, and sat down with his arms across the back of it.

Carrie looked up at him shyly. She offered him the other half of her scone.

Mick shook his head. "No thanks. Just had a big bowl of porridge. It's sticking to my ribs," he said, patting his stomach.

Carrie pushed her plate away and pulled a notebook and pen from her purse. "Look, Mick, I would like to ask you some personal questions."

Anyone else and he would have stood up and walked out. But not her. He could deny her nothing.

"Fire away," he said amiably.

"What was it like growing up with a mother who was a matchmaker?"

Mick laughed. He hadn't expected that; he thought she'd ask him something more personal. Like why he never came back. Like why he hadn't offered her a divorce.

"It was fun," he answered. "My mother was a wonderful woman who believed in love. She was always fixing people up or helping them with their problems in their relationships. People came from all over to ask her for relationship advice."

"Like an agony aunt?" Carrie asked.

"Exactly," Mick said with a smile at the memory of it. Everyone had loved his mother.

"Your home must have been overrun," Carrie said.

Mick's mood quickly shifted. "No, it wasn't. She bought this building back in the 80s and people came here. No one called to the house."

Carrie's eyebrows knitted together in confusion. "Oh?"

He shook his head and looked at his tea in the cup. "No. My father was a drinker. He drank every single day of his short life. And he made life hell for anyone around him."

"Oh, Mick, I'm so sorry," she said.

"It was a long time ago. He died before my mother," he said, full of ambivalence. He'd made peace with it. He couldn't change it.

"Their marriage wasn't happy?" she asked, her voice barely above a whisper.

She trod on dangerous ground. He regarded her for a moment, wondering if it was the reporter who was asking the question. Deciding it was Carrie, he answered, "My mother loved him, though God knows why, and she would never leave him. But no, it wasn't a happy union."

"Is that why you don't drink?" she asked.

"Yes."

There was a moment of silence as they took a sip of their tea.

Mick spoke. "Ma was able to match anyone up, but she failed miserably for herself. The gift doesn't work for the matchmaker."

Carrie flinched as if she'd been burned. "I guess not."

He sighed; he could have worded that better.

"What do you mean about the gift? Can you tell me more about that?" Carrie's open vulnerability just evidenced moments ago was immediately replaced with professionalism.

"There are some people who have a natural ability to paint, sing, or have a green thumb," he explained. "This is like that. It's just something we're good at. It can't be explained because it is what it is."

The interview carried on for another half hour and Mick didn't want it to end. But Carrie began to shuffle her papers like she was wrapping things up.

Looking around the café and at the street outside the window, he saw there was no one around. He might never get an opportunity like this again. It seemed as good a time as any, and it was long overdue.

"Carrie, I want to apologize for what happened between us all those years ago," he said quietly.

"Mick, you might remember that it was my idea to get married," she said. "There's nothing to apologize for."

Mick blinked. "What?"

"I said you don't need to apologize, that it was my idea to get married," she said helpfully.

"Oh yes, right," he said. "I meant I wanted to apologize for what happened after I left," he said softly.

"Nothing happened after you left," she said.

"That's what I mean," he said.

They were both quiet for a moment. This was difficult, and he hoped the apology wasn't too late.

"Do you remember what I said to you on the phone right before I went back to Ireland?" he asked.

Carrie glanced away, looking out at the empty street. She shrugged. "Not off the top of my head."

He wondered if that was true. "I told you I would come back," he said.

"Oh that," Carrie said, looking at him. She blinked and looked away again. "We all say things we don't mean. Besides, you had just lost your mother. You weren't in the right mind."

Mick shook his head. "I intended to come back," he said softly. He stared at his teacup.

"Look, it doesn't matter, that's all in the past," Carrie said hurriedly. She stood up, bumping the table, the cup wobbling on its saucer, cold tea sloshing over the sides.

Mick reached out for her and took hold of her wrist. "It matters to me. Don't leave, Carrie. Let me explain."

Carrie didn't sit back down. Instead, she smiled with a smile that didn't reach her eyes and said, "Look, Mick, you're off the hook. We did something reckless and foolish in our youth. It's not like we need to keep dragging it over the coals. You don't owe me an apology. You don't owe me anything." She picked up her things and left.

"Carrie," he said, his voice trailing off into the space she left behind.

How did he explain to her that the reason he'd never returned was that there wasn't just one reason, there had been many?

The unexpected death of his mother had turned everything upside down. After the blur of the wake and funeral, when it was all over and he was left alone, he not only had become numb, but he became inert as well. When he wasn't mourning over his mother, he was pining away for Carrie.

Grief had prevented him from getting in touch with her initially. But it was his stupid ideas that prevented him from getting in touch with her at all once he came out of that initial fugue of grief. He thought it had been too long. And then he'd thought about what he'd done. He'd married her for his own selfish reasons and then left her without getting in touch with her. In the end, he came to the conclusion that Carrie Fields was better off without him.

When the time came to start planning the first matchmaking festival after his mother's death, the townspeople wondered if it would go on. It was the O'Donovan sisters that had approached Mick about carrying on the tradition. In the beginning, he had balked, but those sisters wouldn't take no for an answer. Kept going on about the importance of tradition, keeping memories alive, and the festival being the lifeblood of the town. In the end, he caved in to their demands. Looking back, he supposed it was the sisters' way of pulling him back to the land of the living. But to his bitter regret, he'd returned to the land of the living without his mother and most importantly, without the woman he'd loved: Carrie.

CHAPTER ELEVEN

CARRIE RUSHED OUT OF the café, the need for air great, and the need for some distance between her and Mick even greater. The last thing she needed or wanted was his pity. She was not someone who needed to be pitied. His apology, though seemingly heartfelt, had left her feeling hollow.

She stood out on the main road that ran through the village. Hopefully, a walk would clear her head.

The realization that she was still in love with Mick had blindsided her. The feelings she had once had for him had been dormant, buried deep, but upon seeing him once again after all this time, those feelings had burst forth to the surface. It was painful, there was no denying that.

Distraction, that's what she needed. Carrie looked around the town, starting to appreciate its charm. The village was just beginning to come to life. Shops opened, doors were unlocked, and shutters raised. People began to emerge from their houses.

Carrie walked over to the square that stood in the center of the town. There were trees lining the square with benches running the perimeter. In the middle of the square was a bronze statue and she went to investigate it up close. The figure was that of a woman, a tall woman with shoulder-length hair. The sculptor had been able to capture the warmth and humor of the woman's smile.

Carrie read the plaque below the statue:

In honor of Bridie Foley, third-generation matchmaker of Kilcornan.

Wife, mother, and friend.

'Above all things, I believe in love.'

Mick's mother.

Carrie's attention was distracted by raised voices across from the square. The butcher had stepped out of his shop and called out to a woman walking toward him. In his hands was a package wrapped in brown paper and tied with string.

"Mrs. Carey! I've got your pork chops for you. Trimmed with just a bit of fat for flavor," he said, handing the woman the package.

"Ah, you're very good, Johnnie," she said, accepting the package and putting it into the canvas bag on her arm.

The butcher nodded and the two of them fell into general conversation.

At the top of the town, the bell rang in the tower of the town's only church, and a small group of elderly people made their way up the road for daily Mass.

Despite it being a sunny April day, there was a bit of a nip in the air, and Carrie pulled her cardigan closer around her.

As she walked along, she nodded to a few people that seemed familiar to her, ones she'd seen in passing since her arrival a few days ago. Not in any particular hurry, she paused at some of the shop windows to admire the hats and the dresses. There was one window that was all boarded up. Peering inside, she could see a few abandoned-looking desks. A couple of newspapers lay on the floor. Carrie took a step back and read the overhead sign. *Kilcornan Weekly*, it read. There was a faded handwritten sign on the door: "Final day of business May 8th." It looked as if it had been closed for a while. Through the grimy window, she could see that dust covered everything.

Carrie took a final look, frowning, and walked on. Newspapers were an important part of the fabric of everyday life. Her parents were avid newspaper readers. In the house she'd grown up in, Sundays were dedicated to church and then home with a box of glazed donuts, the papers, and lots of tea.

This was Mick's home. A home she would love to have gotten to know better had the circumstances been different. But they weren't. In less than two weeks, she'd be heading back to her own home.

She looked up and spotted Charlotte heading into the café. She tried not to let it bother her, but it did.

Quickly she headed back to the Caherdavin Arms, determined to put Mick and his charming town way out of her mind.

Kathy was up and walking around the room with her hair turbaned in a towel.

"Where have you been?" she asked when Carrie entered the room and threw her purse onto her bed.

"Interview with Mick Foley," Carrie said.

"How did it go?"

"Good," Carrie lied.

"Ronan was telling me about all the activities that are going to be taking place for the festival. It sounds like a lot of fun," Kathy said, plugging in the hairdryer near the desk.

"Really?" Carrie asked, trying to feign interest.

Kathy pulled the towel from her head and gave her hair a quick towel dry before dragging a brush through it. "I thought it might be fun to join in."

"Go ahead," Carrie said.

Kathy looked pointedly at Carrie. "I meant for both of us, with Ronan and—" she frowned. "What's wrong?"

The tears came forward in a torrent, and Carrie collapsed on the edge of her bed, putting her head into her hands.

Kathy sat down on her own bed, across from her friend. "What happened? Tell me!"

Carrie sniffed, pulled a tissue from her purse, wiped her eyes, and blew her nose. Then she poured forth her story. She told Kathy everything.

Kathy didn't say anything at first, just sat there with her mouth hanging wide open.

In the end, Kathy finally said, "I'm stunned. I don't know what to say. You've been married all this time to Mick Foley, and you never said a word?"

"I couldn't. What we did was illegal at the time. It probably still is," Carrie explained. She was a little hazy on the laws surrounding this. "I don't want to get deported."

Kathy laughed. "You wouldn't get deported from your own country, silly! You'd just go to prison or something."

Carrie paled and tried not to panic. "You can't tell anyone."

Kathy rushed to reassure her. "I won't. I promise. You know I'm a great secret keeper."

That much was true, much to Carrie's relief. She could count on her best friend's discretion.

"To keep that a secret all this time," Kathy said, reaching over and giving Carrie's hand a quick squeeze. "That must have been a great burden."

Carrie nodded as her eyes welled up with tears again.

"I know you tend to be impulsive, Carrie, and this really tops everything else you've done, but why did you do it?"

Carrie said nothing, just bit her lip.

Kathy nodded knowingly. "You had feelings for him."

Carrie looked away, her eyes welling up again.

"Oh, Carrie," Kathy said in sympathy.

Kathy pressed her lips together. "But he did apologize, and you said he seemed happy to see you."

"But he never came back," Carrie protested.

"And he never asked you for a divorce, either," Kathy remarked.

"What does that matter?" Carrie asked.

"Because it would seem if he wanted to move on from you, he would have contacted you and asked for a divorce," Kathy pointed out.

"And I didn't ask him for one either," Carrie answered.

"Do you want one?"

Carrie laughed a hollow laugh. "That's the ridiculous thing. No, I don't want a divorce, but I suppose I need to move on with my life."

"Can I say something?" Kathy said.

"Sure."

"Do you remember when my mother died?" Kathy asked.

That question came out of nowhere, but of course Carrie remembered. Kathy had taken it hard at the time, and Carrie had worried about her friend. She had seemed so lost.

Kathy looked thoughtful, as if she had been transported back in time. "It took me a year to get my bearings. I was incapable of focusing for that year after Mom died. I felt like I'd been hit by a train."

"I know, I remember."

"It was you and David that helped me get through it."
Carrie smiled at her friend.

"Grief is such a funny thing. You just don't know how it's going to hit you until it does. Maybe you could cut him some slack. You don't know what kind of place he was in after his mother's death. He may have been physically and emotionally unable to get in touch with you."

Carrie sighed. She hadn't even thought of that. She had only thought of it from her perspective. "But there might have been some point in the last ten years where he could have reached out to me." Sympathetic by nature, she wasn't ready to let him off the hook.

"Maybe by the time he came out of his mourning, he figured it was too late," Kathy suggested.

Carrie shrugged.

"Before we leave, you're going to have to have a heart-to-heart with him. If he's not interested or never had feelings for you, then you might want to consider a divorce. You've put your life on hold long enough."

"I suppose you're right," Carrie said with a feeling of dread in her stomach. It was a conversation that had to happen, even if she didn't like the outcome. Even if it was the end of her marriage. And her dream of him.

Enough about her and Mick. "Have you heard from David?" Carrie asked.

The smile immediately disappeared from Kathy's face. Her mouth puckered like she was sucking on a lemon, and she said, "No, I haven't."

Carrie frowned. "I thought he was texting you non-stop."

"Um, yeah, for the first few days, then he must have gotten bored, because the last text I had from him said, 'Take all the time you need.' Now what exactly does that mean?" Kathy demanded.

Carrie looked at her, not comprehending. "I think it means just what it says. You told him you wanted a break, and it sounds like he's going to respect your decision," she said.

Kathy rolled her eyes. "I at least thought he'd fight for me! Protest. Beg me to come home or something," she said, picking imaginary lint off her bathrobe.

"Well, give him time. It's only been a few days."

When Kathy didn't say anything, Carrie changed the subject again. "What are your plans today?"

"Ronan and I are going up to County Donegal," Kathy answered. "He wants to show me around."

Carrie raised an eyebrow. "He seems nice . . ."

"He knows about my situation with David," Kathy answered. "We had a long talk. He knows exactly where he stands. That this is just temporary. Because please, I need another relationship like I need a hole in my head."

"Okay, Kath, but just be careful. I don't want to see either of you get hurt," Carrie said.

Kathy gave a dismissive wave with her hand. "I'll be fine, don't worry."

But sometimes Carrie couldn't help but worry.

"What about you? Do you want to come with us?" Kathy asked, tilting her head. "It might take your mind off things."

Carrie shuddered. She could think of better things to do than be the third wheel. "I have to work. I'm going to find a nice quiet place for me and my trusty laptop and finish a couple of articles I was working on before we left home. And then I'm going to interview more of the couples who got married after meeting here at the festival and are still together."

"That sounds romantic!" Kathy practically gushed.

"Maybe."

The second couple that Carrie had arranged to meet and interview for her article was a younger couple, around Carrie's age, named Jerry and Margaret Mullane. They had met at the Kilcornan Matchmaking Festival just five years before. Carrie didn't want to impose on Sarah again with the use of the conservatory and when Margaret suggested the café, Carrie hesitated. The last thing she wanted was to run into Mick. Or worse, for him to think that she was stalking him.

It was agreed that they would meet at a restaurant just outside of town. It was a quaint place with painted chairs and tables in different colors of blue, white, red, green, and yellow. Floral curtains repeating the same colors hung over the windows, and there was a big slate board listing the menu and the day's specials. Carrie ordered a grilled panini and a cup of tea, and the couple ordered toasted sandwiches, apple tart, and a pot of tea. The June sun shone brightly through the windows. Overall, the whole effect of the room was one of cheerfulness.

Jerry and Margaret Mullane sat next to each other on the other side of the table. They currently lived in County Tipperary, on the farm that Jerry had inherited. Margaret's belly was swollen; she was due with their first child in four weeks.

The interview went off course several times during the meeting, not because of any malicious intent on the part of the Mullanes, but more due to the curiosity of Margaret Mullane. But Carrie reined her back in each time.

"No one can quite believe that the matchmaking festival is going to be featured in an American newspaper. How exciting!" Margaret gushed.

"It's going to make a great article," Carrie said. She understood now why they called them human interest stories because they sure were interesting!

"What do you think of Kilcornan so far?" Jerry asked.

"It's very charming," Carrie said truthfully.

Margaret went to ask something else, but Carrie cut her off politely. She thought Margaret would make a good interviewer herself, so deft were her questions. She'd turned the tables without Carrie ever realizing it.

"First, I'd like to thank you both for agreeing to meet with me and allowing me to ask you some questions for the article in *The Philly Chronicle*," she said. She glanced briefly through her notes. "Can you explain to me how you first met? The circumstances?" Carrie asked.

Jerry and Margaret looked at each other and laughed. Margaret took the lead. "I'd come to the festival with my girlfriend. We'd heard about it, and we thought, why not? We'd had no luck with dating or even online dating. We figured we had nothing to lose."

"As for me, I was just tagging along with a friend," Jerry said. "Although I have to admit that I was curious."

"My girlfriend talked me into signing up for the services of the matchmaker. I didn't know what to expect. He asked us both a few basic questions, we filled out a form, and then twenty-four hours later, he said to me, 'I've got someone I'd like you to meet.'"

Jerry picked up the thread. "I hadn't even signed up for the matchmaking service. But I'd arrived in town a few days before Margaret, and my friend had signed up for the service. I spoke to Mick a few times, just about general stuff. And then one day he asked me if I would be interested in meeting someone. He knew a girl who would be perfect for me, he said."

Jerry shrugged. "And I was like, okay, why not?" Then he looked at Margaret with a smile. "And Mick was right, she is perfect for me."

Margaret glowed from his adoration and quite possibly from the pregnancy as well.

"Tell me about your proposal." Carrie encouraged.

Jerry and Margaret looked at each other and laughed again. Carrie noted that after only five years together, this couple was totally in sync.

Jerry spoke up first. "We'd been seeing each other for a year after the festival. I knew this woman was the one for me." Margaret beamed when he said this. "I'd made it very clear that if we were ever to get married, she'd have to move up to Tipperary, as that's where the farm is."

Margaret interrupted. "It's a beautiful place; the views are just to die for."

Jerry smiled proudly and picked up his story. "We'd just come back from going to the festival, this time as a couple—"

"We had such a wonderful time," Margaret gushed. "All the dancing!"

"We stopped back in Tipperary on our way home. I took her to our parish graveyard next to our church," he said.

Carrie had seen the graveyards of Ireland: old, with ancient Celtic crosses and tombstones covered with moss and lichen and names that had been worn down by time and weather.

"I showed her the family plot where generations of Mullanes are buried."

"And I was thinking, okay, this is nice, but why are you showing me this?" Margaret laughed as she recalled the event.

Jerry looked affectionately at Margaret. "And then I said to her, 'So Margaret, what do you say? Do your bones want to lie next to mine someday?'"

Carrie raised her eyebrows. Not the most romantic proposal, but it had worked because here they sat, wearing a pair of matching wedding bands and with a baby on the way. She'd give him points for originality.

Carrie turned to Margaret and asked, "Did you think it was romantic?"

Margaret smiled and nodded. "I did. Although to some, it might seem morbid, a proposal in a graveyard. But the fact that he wanted to be buried next to me was romantic, because I read into it that he wanted me for life. Not just for now, but for forever." Her eyes misted over. She fanned her face with her hand and said, "Sorry, the hormones are crazy with me."

Jerry covered her hand with his and smiled.

Carrie remembered her short-term relationship with Mick. A hollow feeling filled her, and she felt sad. What little bit she had had was in no way a comparison to what this lucky couple had together.

Chapter Twelve

Mick hurried to the community center for the start of the couples' cook-off. He kept his eyes open for Carrie as he hadn't seen her since the previous morning. And since then, she'd occupied his every waking thought.

"Oh, Mick! Mick, wait up!" called a familiar voice.

"Give me strength, Lord," Mick muttered under his breath. He wasn't a swearing man, but he was seriously thinking of taking it up.

Charlotte dashed toward him. "Are you heading to the couples' cook-off?" she asked.

As much as he wanted to, he couldn't lie to her. "I am."

"I'll walk with you," she said.

Charlotte talked nonstop on the way to the community center. And even though it was a short walk, Mick had a headache by the time they arrived.

Although Mick was in charge of the activities, he delegated different events to different people. Sarah Caherdavin ran the cook-off; she had for years.

Mick stood at the door and surveyed the place, a beehive of activity. All the chairs had been removed in favor of makeshift workstations, placed in rows in the middle of the room. Most of them were occupied by eager couples. Volunteers ran back and forth doing last-minute things under Sarah's expert direction.

"Charlotte, would you do me a favor?" he asked.

She beamed. "Anything."

"Can you see if they need any help in the kitchen?"

"Sure thing," she said, and she hurried off.

Sarah approached him carrying a clipboard.

"How's it going?" he asked.

"Good," she said, glancing at her watch. "We're on track to begin on time."

Mick nodded. "Full house?"

"Not quite," she said with a small frown. "We could use a few extra couples."

"Let me see if I can round some up," he volunteered. He turned to leave and spotted Carrie walking through the door.

Sarah placed her hand on Mick's arm. "Hold on, Mick." She waved Carrie over. "Carrie! I'm so happy you decided to come."

Carrie avoided looking at Mick and said to Sarah, "This looks like a lot of fun."

"I'm glad you think so, because we're short some couples and I've assigned you and Mick to table number nineteen," Sarah said briskly, scribbling their names down on her sign-up sheet.

Carrie paled. "But I don't know how to cook!"

Mick suppressed a grin by putting his finger over his mouth.

Sarah smiled. "That's even better! Think of all the fun you'll have."

"I could step in for Carrie," Charlotte volunteered from Mick's side. Mick did a double-take. Where had she come from? She had just gone off to the kitchen. As if reading his mind, Charlotte said to him, "They don't need any help in the kitchen."

"Charlotte, that's lovely of you to offer, but as this is Carrie's first year at the festival, and hopefully not her last," Sarah said with a wink, "we'll let her try it out."

"Maybe we could find another fella for Carrie," Charlotte pushed.

"No time for that. Come on, Carrie," Mick said.

"Here's your badges," Sarah said. She peeled the backings off of two badges, stuck them on their shirts, and pushed them in the direction of their assigned workstation.

"She comes across as real demure and sweet, but she's quite forceful," Carrie muttered.

Mick laughed. Ignoring her protests, he said, "Come on, we don't want to be disqualified for being late." He started back toward the makeshift island they'd been assigned to, and he realized she wasn't following him. He turned around and called, "I don't bite. Where's your sense of adventure? It'll give you another dimension to your story."

Carrie didn't have a chance to respond before Sarah's voice came over the PA system. She stood in the middle of the floor with a mic, introducing herself and laying out the rules.

There were about twenty workstations set up in all. Sarah held a big box and went around the room to each station, having each couple pull out a sealed envelope with their assigned recipe inside.

Mick hoped for something easy, as he wasn't much of a cook, either. Hopefully, Carrie's cooking skills were better than his.

The first couple must have picked something difficult, because they groaned. The second couple threw up their hands in a high five and were all smiles with their pick. Mick held his breath when the organizers reached them.

He nodded to Carrie. "Go ahead, Miss America, you do the honors."

She nodded, drew in a deep breath, and thrust her hand in the box. As she felt around inside, her eyes shifted upwards to the left and she bit her lip. She pulled out a sealed envelope, opened it, and looked at the directions inside.

"Oh boy." She winced.

Mick held his breath. "What is it?"

Carrie frowned. "Banoffee pie. What's that?"

"A nice dessert. Rich," he answered. "Okay, let's read the recipe. And try not to panic."

"Can it be made in a microwave?" she asked, practically wailing.

"I doubt it."

They hunched over their recipe together, their shoulders touching. Distracted by her arm touching his and the smell of her perfume, Mick must have read the first line of the directions at least three times. He was overwhelmed by the desire to just be with her. To take her by the hand and lead her out of this place to somewhere more private. He swallowed hard and tried to concentrate.

"We have to make our own caramel?" Carrie asked, pointing to an instruction. "And what is condensed milk?"

Mick scratched the back of his head and realized he didn't know, either. They might be in a bit of trouble. But he didn't care if they came in last place. He just wanted to be with her.

He straightened up to get to work. There was a time limit. And he had to put some physical distance between her and him. She was doing his head in.

"Okay, where do we find the ingredients?" Carrie asked, looking up at him with her eyes big and round.

"Uh, what?" he asked, dragging his eyes away from hers.

"The ingredients?" Carrie repeated.

"Oh, yeah," Mick looked around and saw other couples going into the community center's kitchen. "Come on, let's do this."

Side by side they walked through the swinging doors of the kitchen. There were tables set up, laden with ingredients.

Jerry and Margaret Mullane were volunteering behind the tables. Margaret Mullane looked like she was about to pop any minute with that baby. Mick felt a bit a pride when he looked at them; after all, it was he who had set them up.

"All your mixing bowls, measuring equipment, and baking trays or pans will be found at your station. Grab your ingredients and let's get you started," Jerry instructed.

Mick and Carrie scanned up and down the supply table.

Margaret approached them. "Give me your recipe and I'll gather your ingredients."

"Carrie? Recipe, please," Mick said.

Carrie looked at him. "I thought you had it."

"You didn't bring it with you?" Mick asked.

Carrie shook her head.

Margaret laughed. "Thank goodness it's just a recipe and not a baby!"

Carrie reddened and Mick said, "I'll go get it."

He returned in no time to find Carrie and Margaret chatting away like old friends. He handed the recipe to Margaret.

With their arms full of ingredients, Mick and Carrie returned to their workstation.

Carrie scanned the recipe. "Okay, we need to make the base." Her forehead creased. "It calls for ten to twelve digestives and melted butter." She looked up at Mick. "What are digestives?"

He pulled the sleeve of cookies off the table, opened it with his pocketknife, pulled out a cookie and handed it to Carrie.

Carrie studied the cookie, a plain medallion the color of sand. She took a bite. "Oh, kind of like a graham cracker. Hmm. Nice." She popped the rest of the cookie in her mouth.

"Okay, it says we have to crush the digestives, mix them with the melted butter, and put them in the bottom of a pan, flattening them with a fork," Mick read from the recipe.

Carrie nodded. "I know how to do this. When I was a kid, my mother used to make cheesecake, and the base was very similar."

She took over, putting a liberal amount of butter in a pan and setting it on the hot plate.

"Now keep an eye on that, and don't let the butter burn," she directed.

"I thought you said you didn't know how to cook," Mick said, taking a wooden spoon and stirring the butter around.

She laughed. "I don't. But melting the butter was always my job when my mother baked."

"It sounds nice," he said, remembering his own mother.

Carrie looked startled for a minute. "It was." She didn't look at him as she laid out the digestives on the counter.

She used a rolling pin to crush the cookies. Once finished, she poured the crushed biscuits into a mixing bowl. "How's the butter coming?"

Mick looked into the pot and removed it from the hot plate. "It's melted."

"Okay, let's get this show on the road."

Mick added the melted butter to the crushed digestives as Carrie mixed them with a fork. Once that was done, she handed the bowl to Mick.

"Here, just pour it into the pan and pat it flat against the bottom."

Mick did as he was told and had it sorted in less than five minutes. It had to chill in the refrigerator for another ten.

While they waited, Mick said casually, "We seem to be doing okay here."

Carrie snorted. "Don't jinx us, we're not finished yet."

Quietly, they went about their work. Carrie turned to him and asked, "Wouldn't you rather have done this with Charlotte?"

Mick scowled. "No, why would I?"

"I just thought—"

"That we were a couple?" Mick asked. He had to make this very clear to her. "We're not. Although in a parallel world, Charlotte thinks we are."

"Why don't you tell her?" Carrie said.

"I have, but she doesn't listen," Mick said, his voice tinged with exasperation.

Carrie laughed. "Your very own groupie!"

Mick winced.

"Have you had a lot of girlfriends?" Carrie asked out of the blue, surprising him.

"I've dated. But nothing serious," he said. "Even if I wasn't already married, they wouldn't have worked out anyway."

"Why not?"

"Mostly it was incompatibility issues—"

"Like what?"

"I don't know. The one girl lived in Dublin. Me moving there or her moving here wasn't an option. Then there was one that wanted me to get a real job," he said with a laugh.

Carrie looked horrified. "She did not!"

Mick nodded. "She did. Felt me being a matchmaker didn't present the right 'look.'"

"You're better off without her," Carrie said firmly.

"Thanks, Mam," he said.

"Never mind, carry on," she said.

"And there was one girlfriend who was a committed vegan, who said I'd have to give up the meat for the relationship to continue," he said. "Turns out I liked steak a lot more than I liked her."

Carrie laughed. "You're terrible!"

"But most of all, they just weren't for me? Do you know what I mean? Where you know that another person is 'the one?'"

"Yes, I know," Carrie said, her voice low.

"I have lots of women I consider very good friends, but I wouldn't want to form a relationship with them," Mick said. "Other than your disastrous blind dates, have you had any serious relationships? Since I left?"

"No," Carrie said, her face reddening. "I decided to put my career first."

"You'd rather curl up with a newspaper than curl up with a man?" he teased, looking at her pointedly.

Carrie stretched her neck and rolled her shoulders. "Never mind what I want to curl up with. Let's get back to what we have to do."

Mick glanced at the clock. "That base should be chilled by now."

"I suppose we should tackle the caramel," Carrie said hesitantly.

Mick shrugged. "Sure, why not? How hard can it be?"

"Um, pretty hard?" Carrie said.

Simultaneously, they leaned over to read the recipe and ended up banging their heads together. Both immediately straightened up, and each put a hand on their forehead and winced.

"Well, that hurt," Carrie said.

"Sure did." Mick agreed. For someone who appeared to be all softness and curves, her head was as hard as a rock. "You first." He gestured toward the recipe. Once her head was down, he leaned in to try to read over her shoulder, but Carrie straightened up, banging the back of her head into his chin.

"Oh, I'm so sorry!" she said. "I just wanted to tell you it says to be careful not to burn the sugar or overcook it, or it will be too grainy."

"Does it say anything about banging heads together?" he asked, rubbing his chin.

"No, it doesn't."

They set about opening a can of condensed milk, pouring it into a small pot, adding sugar and bringing the mixture to a boil. They both reached for the wooden spoon to stir the ingredients together to make the caramel. Carrie retreated and said with a smile, "You go ahead, Mick, I did the base."

"Are you sure? Because I don't mind."

As soon as the caramel thickened, Carrie let out a squeal of delight. "I can't believe we made caramel!"

Mick gazed at her, full of admiration. She was so full of joy at her success that he found himself smiling.

After he poured the caramel over the base of crushed biscuits, Carrie carefully sliced two bananas and laid them on top of the caramel. The last thing that needed to be done was the cream topping.

Mick poured a small jug of cream into the bowl and added a few tablespoons of icing sugar to it. He set the bag of icing sugar and the empty cream container on the counter. He handed the electric mixer to Carrie. "Whip it up."

Carrie set the mixer on high, and the vibration of the bowl sent the empty jug clattering to the floor. Mick knelt to pick it up. As he did, he heard Carrie gasp, "Oh no!"

He looked up just as the open bag of sugar, now on its side, dumped its powdery contents all over his head.

Mick coughed, licked his lips and blinked his eyes. He felt like human cotton candy.

Carrie's hands flew to her face in shock and horror, and she laughed. "I am so sorry!" She grabbed the dish towel and vigorously wiped off his face and his hair as if he were a dog that had just come in from a muddy field.

When she was finished, she stepped back and waited for his reaction, holding her breath.

"You know, Carrie, you're downright dangerous in the kitchen," he said. He would have winked at her to reassure her, but he couldn't, because his eyelashes were sticking together.

After a shower that required two washings with shampoo to get all the icing sugar out, Mick helped Rosemary unload some boxes from the storage room. He never ceased to be impressed by her strength. Their mother used to say she was big-boned like a man and had the strength of ten men. She lifted and moved boxes with ease, never breaking a sweat.

"Thanks, Mick," she said. She removed her heavy work gloves and threw them on top of one of the boxes.

"Now, why don't you tell me what's going on with that American reporter?"

It was just like Rosemary to get straight to the point.

"What do you mean?" he asked, stalling for time.

Rosemary rolled her eyes. "Don't play cute with me, Mick. Spit it out." She paused, then said, "It's all over town how you two did a cooking demo together."

"She's nice, and she's doing an article for her paper."

Rosemary raised her eyebrows and waited. And for some unknown reason, Mick told his sister everything. How he had married Carrie all those years ago.

For a minute, Rosemary said nothing. And then she put her hands on her hips and pursed her lips, reminiscent of what she used to do when they were younger, and she was in charge and about to rain a whole lot of hurt down on him. Mick practically flinched, waiting for the blowback.

"What's wrong with you?"

He didn't reply right away, unsure if she required an answer. Sometimes when she was on a tear, it was best just to stay quiet.

"We were foolish and reckless and young. I didn't want to leave America. I wanted to get to know her better."

"I'm not talking about that!" Rosemary said, clearly annoyed. "You married her, left her when Ma died, and you never got in touch with her after that? I can't believe you."

Mick shrugged, knowing he had no good answer. "I always thought I would go back for her."

"When?" Rosemary asked. Mick did not miss the anger in her voice. "When she was forty and too old to have children of her own?"

Rosemary pressed her lips together tightly and Mick was alarmed.

"Don't start swearing, Rosemary. You left that life of foul, colorful language behind you years ago. Don't fall off the wagon because of me."

She muttered something under her breath. Whether it was an expletive or not, Mick couldn't be sure. And whether it constituted falling off the wagon, he couldn't be sure of that, either. And besides, who was he to judge?

"Before that girl leaves, you're going to talk to her about divorce, and then you're going to make it happen," Rosemary said. "And if you don't, I'll wrap my hands around your bloody neck!"

She stormed out and slammed the door behind her.

Mick didn't want to divorce Carrie. But maybe his sister was right. Maybe he had held Carrie back. Maybe it was time to let her go so she could get on with her life.

Chapter Thirteen

T HE FOLLOWING MORNING, CARRIE noticed a post-card beneath the hotel-room door. It stated that the elevator was back in service. Sarah had signed her name and added a smiley face.

Once dressed, she made her way down to the lobby and immediately noticed Arthur on the ottoman. He was conscious! Maybe morning was his best time of the day. But he regarded her with indifference.

"Oh, it's nice to see you're awake," she said, walking over to him. The dog's tail thumped slowly against the ottoman. Even that seemed to be a lot of effort for him. Carrie sat down next to him, and the dog lay back on his side, lifted his forepaw, and groaned.

Carrie laughed, reached out and rubbed his side. The dog's eyes were already at half-mast by the second stroke. She laughed again. "Boy, it doesn't take you much to fall asleep." His eyes closed and he soon settled into a contented snore.

"I was looking for some conversation, but I guess you're not interested in being a sounding board," Carrie said to the sleeping dog.

"Are you talking to my dog?" Sarah asked with a laugh as she entered the room.

Carrie looked up quickly and blushed at being caught talking to a sleeping dog. And one she hardly knew. And who wasn't interested.

Carrie laughed to cover up her embarrassment. "I know, it's silly."

Sarah gave her a warm smile. "Not really. I used to talk to him all the time; he was a great listener. Now he can't keep his eyes open."

They regarded the sleeping dog for a minute and then Sarah asked, "Did you enjoy the cook-off?"

"I did. And I've never had banoffee pie before, so it was a win-win," Carrie said.

"Will you be going to the GAA field for the race today?" Sarah asked.

"I am. Just tagging along with Kathy and Ronan and Eddie," she said, adding for emphasis, "I will not be participating." She wanted to make that clear.

"No worries," Sarah said. "I don't run that. Mick has run the race himself for years."

Carrie was glad to hear that. That meant they couldn't be ambushed and set up as they'd been at the cook-off. Although she'd loved spending the time with Mick, it had led to her daydreaming about the two of them together in *their* kitchen, cooking and baking together. And those kinds of thoughts were dangerous.

"I'll see you later," Carrie said.

"Enjoy yourself. That race is so much fun."

She waved goodbye and headed out to catch up with Kathy, Ronan, and Eddie.

The GAA field was located behind the old stone church and the cemetery at the top of the town. As Carrie walked up the hill toward the church making small talk with Eddie, she noted the building's steeple and bell tower. It looked like a scene from a postcard. The church appeared to be watching over the town below.

Carrie wondered about the couples' activity due to take place that afternoon. Kathy had seemed excited about it. Said it was going to be a lot of fun. It was some kind of race, but that was all Carrie knew. Maybe a three-legged race or a wheelbarrow race. Lots of other people were walking up the hill as well. It must be a big event, she mused. It was a couples' activity, but Eddie hadn't asked her so she figured she was off the hook.

They followed the crowd through a gate in a cement-block wall that ran along the front of the field. The wall had been painted red and white for the festival. Inside was a pitch with goalie nets at either end and portable aluminum bleachers flanking each side. At the far end of the field hung a banner in front of the goalie net that read, "Carry Her across the Threshold." And from one end of the end zone to the other was strung a finish-line tape.

It couldn't be what she thought it meant. That would simply be too crazy. Most likely it was just a play on words, she told herself.

There was a crowd gathering at the end zone nearest her, and they made their way through the throng of couples, all laughing and smiling. She spotted Mick hanging out and talking to the O'Donovan sisters.

"Hello, Carrie," Mick said.

"I see you got the sugar out of your hair," she said.

"It only took two shampoos." He grinned.

Maeve O'Donovan stood on one side of Mick and her sister on the other. Maeve wore a tan-and-green hunting jacket over her tweed skirt. "So, you've come to partake in one of the activities, is it?"

Before Carrie could explain that she was just a spectator, Maeve's sister Millie piped in. "Good for you! It's a lot of fun!" Millie was similarly attired in a tweed jacket with patches on the elbow.

The sisters looked like they'd be at home with a bunch of duck hunters.

Maeve spoke up. "I won this event back in '49 with Joe John Gilroy, may he rest in peace."

"And I won it two years running in '50 and '51 with Mossie Gilligan," Millie said proudly. She raised her eyes heavenward and exclaimed, "And wherever he is, should he only stay, please God."

"What kind of activity is this, exactly?" Carrie asked.

"It's an event called Carry Her across the Threshold. It's one of our more popular events of the festival," Mick explained.

Judging by the size of the crowd, she believed it.

"What exactly happens here?" Kathy asked with a grin.

Ronan and Eddie looked at each other and laughed.

"It's just as it sounds. The men carry the women down the field, and whoever crosses the finish line first wins!"

He made it sound as simple as a sack race. Carrie thought it sounded a little dangerous.

"Let's see, Kathy and Ronan, I've got you checked, so you can go stand at the starting line," Mick said, scanning the list on his clipboard. He looked up at the starting line, where couples were lined up. "That's everyone, I think."

Kathy giggled, and she and Ronan went off to get in their place.

Mick looked at Carrie and Eddie. "Would you two like to join the race?"

Eddie looked at Carrie from head to toe and said, "I've got a bad back."

"Oh, that's all right, I'm just going to watch," Carrie said.

"That's nonsense!" Maeve cried. She took the clipboard out of Mick's hands. "Mick, show this lovely American girl how it's done here in Kilcornan."

"Give me the starter pistol, Mick," Millie said.

"You're joking, right?" Carrie asked, panic setting in. She didn't want Mick carrying her across the field. Was he crazy? She wasn't exactly a lightweight, and she didn't want to be responsible for any future back problems. And most of all, she didn't want to be embarrassed.

"Come on, it'll be fun. We do this every year," he said easily.

"Every year? How are everyone's backs?" she asked.

"They're fine. Stop worrying," he told her.

Carrie wondered if he was spending too much time in his office. "Look, I'm not doing this. I'm too heavy. I can't have you lifting me across a field!"

Mick scoffed at her statement. "You're not heavy. I got a good look at you. I can do it."

Carrie's eyes knitted together in a scowl. "What do you mean, you got a good look at me?"

Before he could reply, the starter pistol went off, and Mick scooped her up and began running. Suddenly, Carrie was in his arms. She was stunned speechless.

"Oh!" Carrie protested, her eyes wide. "Mick, are you insane?"

"Lockdown unit or just need-to-up-my-meds insane?"

"Either!"

There had to be about thirty other couples running down the field. She spotted Ronan carrying Kathy, the both of them giggling.

"What do I do with my arms?" Carrie asked, her voice high.

"Just put them around my neck!"

Carrie wrapped her arms around his neck as he shifted her up, higher and closer to his chest. He made it look so easy, as if she were as light as a feather. Her head now leaned against his shoulder. Years ago, she used to imagine him holding her. She just hadn't thought it would be while he dashed across a GAA pitch. She craned her neck to look at the other couples. Although Mick had a good position, the competition was fierce.

"This is ridiculous, you know!" Carrie said.

"I know, but it's fun," Mick answered, slightly breathless.

To Carrie, the finish line seemed far away. She hoped Mick would make it.

She eyed the couple nearest to them. The man was tall and skinny, but the woman was short and on the heavy side. The man's face was beet red, and his breath came out in short, sharp bursts. Carrie looked at him with concern.

"Come on, Billy, pick up your pace," yelled his wife, her voice high and shrill.

"Okay, Doreen," the man said amiably. But the opposite happened. He began to slow down. Carrie watched over

Mick's shoulder as the man came to an abrupt halt and sank to his knees and his wife fell out of his arms and rolled onto the ground.

"Billy!" his wife shrieked.

"Oh, no," Carrie said.

"What?" Mick asked.

"A man just dropped his wife. Should we go back and help them?" It seemed rude not to.

"Nah. That was probably Billy and Doreen, that happens every year. Pay no mind to them."

Mick picked up speed. In his eyes was a sense of determination.

"Are you trying to win this race?" Carrie asked.

Keeping his eye on the finish line, Mick huffed, "Yeah, why not?"

"It doesn't seem right somehow," Carrie said.

"I've sat on the sidelines year after year. This year I'm winning!"

"Okay then," Carrie said, not wanting to challenge his determination.

"Besides, when we got married, I never did carry you across the threshold. I'm making up for lost time," he said, his breath labored.

"Stop talking and save your breath," she commanded.

Crowds in the bleachers stood and cheered them all on. It made Carrie smile. Kilcornan certainly was unique. A couple was running along the sidelines and the man stopped, out of breath and unable to go on. His partner didn't hesitate. She picked him up in her arms and started heading toward the finish line, albeit somewhat unsteadily. An uproar of cheers erupted from the crowd.

The finish-line tape was so close that Carrie could see the red hearts stamped across it. By this time Mick's face was red and his brow was damp.

"Oh, wow, we're going to win this!" she exclaimed.

"Of course we are!" Mick cried as he carried her across the threshold, breaking the finish-line tape.

Carrie could hear more cheers from the crowd behind them. Mick set her down and bent over, hands on his knees, drawing in some breaths. She was unsure what to do but felt like she should do something, so she placed her hand on his back until he straightened up. Wasn't that what a wife would do?

As the other competitors and the spectators surged around them, Mick put one arm around Carrie, pulled her to him, and planted a quick, congratulatory kiss on Carrie's lips. So surprised was she that she didn't even close her eyes and was speechless afterward.

"Thanks for being a good sport, Miss America," he whispered to her and winked.

"No problem," she said, her voice shaky. She remained rooted to the spot, caught off-balance by the kiss, even if it was a quick one. It was the spontaneity of it that had taken her by surprise. Mick began to get carried away by the crowd, but he reached for her, took hold of her hand and pulled her closer to him.

"What do we win?" Carrie said.

Mick grinned. "You'll see."

Carrie could only imagine. The throng around them parted as last year's winners approached them.

In the woman's hands was a rhinestone tiara with a veil attached to it.

"Oh, you're kidding me," Carrie said. She looked up at Mick, whose eyes crinkled in the corners.

The woman placed the veil on Carrie's head. Carrie had never worn a veil before, and its hidden meaning made her turn a deep shade of red.

Mick grinned at her. "It suits you."

"Does it?" she asked, unsure.

He nodded and their eyes locked, and Carrie felt something pass between them.

"Yeah, it does," he said softly.

The moment was interrupted by well-wishers dumping a bottle of champagne over Mick's head. He got swallowed up in the crowd, leaving Carrie standing there, wearing a wedding veil.

Chapter Fourteen

Mick knew he should get a move on. The crowning of the King and Queen of Kilcornan was a matter of days away, and he needed to pull the thrones out of storage. Every year, the festival culminated in the crowning of a king and queen on the last night.

Spending time with Carrie had left him thinking. A lot. More than usual. He sat in the office, feet up on his desk, listening to Irish music. The High Kings were playing.

Something had happened at the race yesterday that had unnerved him. As far back as he could remember, the Carrying Her Across the Threshold race had been one of the more popular activities of the festival. It had always looked like fun, and he'd been all for it when the O'Donovan sisters volunteered him to be Carrie's partner. But once the starter pistol went off and he picked Carrie up in his arms, something shifted inside of him. Holding her close to his heart, the smell of her shampoo, her hair brushing against his cheek . . . suddenly, he'd been blindsided by a flurry of emotions that he had not anticipated. It had made him run faster. As if his life depended on it. The urgency to put her down and put some physical distance between him and her overwhelmed him. It was with great relief that he broke through the finish line, the tape winding around them. Carrie had seemed dumbfounded by it all. When they put the wedding veil on her, she looked lovely, and he found himself at a loss for words. Luckily, being doused in champagne had brought him back to his senses. They'd been separated by the crowd and when he looked for her later, she was gone.

Her being here, he wondered if it was an opportunity to recover something that he'd lost. But what if she wasn't interested? She had not given him one signal that showed any interest. And he couldn't discount his past.

Mick turned his thoughts away from Carrie and the confusion he felt and focused on his task of retrieving the thrones. He'd have to bring the two of them out of storage and assess their condition. Sometimes they needed a touch-up, and sometimes the upholstery needed to be refilled. Fortunately, there was a woman in town who could do that quickly if needed. But still, he didn't want to wait until the last moment to do it. Once a couple was crowned king and queen of the festival, that was it until next year. He usually picked the king and queen himself, but between thinking about Carrie and trying to dodge Charlotte Connors, he'd let his duties slide. He decided not to worry about it and just trust the process.

With the end of the festival would also come Carrie's departure. He tapped his pen against his desk. He didn't want her to go. He sighed and leaned back in his chair. Without realizing it, his thoughts had drifted back to Carrie. He gave up and let them lead him where they wanted to go.

His mind raced back and forth over the pros and cons of a relationship with Carrie.

The cons were obvious. She lived three thousand miles away. Relationships were tricky enough without adding an ocean in between. And he'd made the decision years ago while living under his father's roof that he'd never risk becoming the kind of husband Frank Foley had been.

The cons alone appeared insurmountable to him. But then again, there were so many checks on the plus side that Mick didn't know where to start. Carrie Fields was the whole package. She had looks, intelligence, humor, a sense of adventure, and she made him laugh. But it was about more than her ticking off boxes on a checklist. He liked how she made him feel when he was with her. Like life was full of good things and all hopeful possibilities. That he could be someone else—a better version of himself.

He reminded himself that a list of pros and cons was futile if she didn't feel the way about him that he felt about her. He tried not to let that thought depress him.

As if on cue, Carrie appeared in the doorway.

Grateful that she couldn't read his mind, Mick removed his feet from the desk and stood up from his chair.

"Good morning, Carrie," he said.

"Good morning," she said softly.

"Are you all recovered from the race?" he asked.

"I am. It was a lot of fun," she said. "I've brought the veil back. You'll probably need it for next year."

"Sure you don't want to keep it? As a memento?" he asked.

Carrie shook her head. "No thanks."

He was disappointed but tried not to show it. She handed him the veil and he put it on his desk.

"Sit down," he said.

"I was just going to grab a tea. Did you want anything?" she asked, leaning against the doorframe.

Did he want anything? He was beginning to think he did. He wanted to touch her face to see if the skin was as soft as it looked. He wanted to run his fingers through her hair to see if it felt like silk. And most of all, he wanted to kiss those lips of hers properly. A thousand times.

"Mick, I asked if you wanted anything," Carrie said with a smile. "You're lost in your thoughts."

And what thoughts they were! He nodded toward the half-empty, now-gone-cold cup of tea on his desk. "I'm fine. I was going to pull out the thrones for the King and Queen of Kilcornan crowning. Feel like helping?" It was just an invitation to help pull out old furniture, so why was he as nervous as a cat?

"Yeah, sure, maybe you could answer some questions for me, for the article," she said, tapping her finger against the door frame. When he nodded, she said, "I'll be right back."

She disappeared, and Mick thought, of course she was only interested in the interview. Whatever it took to get the story. Dejected, he threw his pen onto the desk, picked up the veil and fingered it. He narrowed his eyes, and memories of their wedding day came back to him. As they often did. Annoyed with himself, he picked the veil up and hung it on the hook on the back of the door so he wouldn't have to look at it.

Once she returned with her beverage in a takeout cup, the tag to the tea bag hanging over the side, the two of them headed to the back of the restaurant to the storage room. Mick unlocked the door and flipped on the light switch. The light illuminated a long and narrow room with all sorts of furniture and boxes piled up against the walls. A path in between all the items led to the back of the storage room, and Mick led the way with Carrie behind him. In the small, confined space of the room, Mick became aware of her perfume. He closed his eyes and drew in a deep breath, committing the scent to memory.

"They're just here in the back," he said over his shoulder to Carrie.

At the back of the room, Mick pulled aside a pair of drop cloths, revealing two throne chairs of ornately carved mahogany with garnet-colored velvet on the seats and the backs.

"Wow! They really are thrones!" Carrie said, clearly impressed.

"I picked up these two chairs years ago from an antique shop, and all I had to do was recover them." He gave them a brief visual inspection, seeing no damage.

Carrie looked at him in surprise. "You recover furniture as well?"

He shook his head and laughed. This was how rumors started. "No, one of the women in town is a seamstress, and she recovered them. I just picked out the fabric, with her guidance of course."

"Oh, of course," Carrie joked. With her cup in hand, she sat down on one of the thrones. She smiled.

"Your throne, Miss America," he said.

"All I need is a scepter and orb!" Carrie crossed her legs at the knee and sipped her tea. Mick joined her by sitting down next to her on the other throne.

They were interrupted by Rosemary in the doorway, who hesitated when she saw them sitting on the thrones.

"Oh, I wondered why the storage-room door was open," she said, looking back and forth between Mick and Carrie. "Hey, do you want me to ask Dennis to transport the chairs over to McAllister's?" she asked. "He's here now."

"If he doesn't mind," Mick said.

Rosemary nodded and regarded the two of them with a grin. "I'll leave you to it!"

"You wanted to ask me some questions?" he asked.

"Here?" she said, peering over the rim of her cup.

Mick shrugged. "Sure, why not? It's private." Secretly, he would have preferred to ask her some questions. To interview her. Suddenly, he needed to know everything about her.

Carrie pulled a notebook and pen from her purse.

She tapped her pen against her teeth and looked up at him and smiled. "Okay. Did you ever get it wrong?"

He frowned at her. "What do you mean?"

"Has a match you've set up not worked out?" she asked.

"Well, sure, nothing is one hundred percent in life," he said.

"Anyone unhappy with their match?" she asked.

"There was one woman, years ago, who wrote to me and complained about the fella I'd matched her up with," Mick recalled. "She said he didn't make a nice cup of tea."

Carrie smiled again but said nothing.

"I told her to cut him some slack, but she wasn't to be denied, said there was no hope for the relationship without a proper cup of tea," Mick told her.

"What happened?"

"She asked for a refund, and I told her to read the fine print," Mick said. "As it is a subjective business with many variables, there are no guarantees and no refunds. But you see, there is just no pleasing some people."

"Maybe not," she said, their eyes locking. Carrie broke eye contact first, bent her head, and stared at her notebook. But she wrote nothing.

"But I would hope your success rate is better than your failure rate," she said.

He almost winced at the word "failure." It felt personal, but he chose to ignore it. "It sure is. If it wasn't, I'd be out of business."

There was a pause between them. Mick leaned forward and rested his elbows on his knees.

"I wasn't a very good husband, was I?" he asked.

Carrie sighed and sipped her tea. "As it was a marriage in name only, it was hard to tell." She added, "I wasn't much of a wife."

"You were a great wife!"

"Why would you say that?" she asked, leaning back against her throne.

"Because it's true. You were so easy to get along with," he said.

A silence fell between them.

"Carrie, my father did not give me a good example of how to be a husband or a father."

Carrie listened.

"He treated my mother badly and as a father, he did the bare minimum."

"Thanks for telling me this," Carrie said.

"I'm afraid of—"

Rosemary reappeared in the doorway, interrupting Mick.

"Dennis will take them over now," she announced.

"All right," Mick said with a hint of irritation in his voice, resentful at the intrusion.

Carrie nodded, put her pen and notebook back in her purse, and slung her purse over her shoulder.

Not wanting to end their conversation on a sour note, he said, "Don't forget about the last couples' activity over at the community center."

"It's not another race, is it?" she asked with a grin.

"Nope, more like a game show."

"Sounds like fun," she said.

"Are you enjoying the festival?" he asked.

"I am!" she enthused. "It's a lot of fun, and I just love the town."

Mick filled with pride. It meant something to him that she loved the town, too.

The following evening, Mick stood backstage with Carrie at the community center. It turned out that Rosemary had signed both him and Carrie up for that evening's event.

"Do you ever get the feeling that we're being set up?" he asked.

She grinned. "There seems to be a conspiracy. Apparently, you're not the only matchmaker in town."

"My job appears to be in danger," he said.

"So what event is this?" she asked, her arms folded across her chest. She wore a jean jacket over a plum-colored T-shirt and a pair of jeans.

"It's called Truth and Dare," he answered.

"You never said anything about truth or dare!" Carrie hissed. "I can't do truth or dare!"

"Truth *and* dare," he corrected.

"Whatever. It doesn't matter, because I can't do it," Carrie said.

"Why not?"

"Why not?" Carrie repeated, her voice rising higher. "I'm a veteran of high-school truth or dare games. An experience from which I've never recovered! Just ask Kathy." Her eyes glittered in the dim backstage lighting.

If she wasn't so serious, she'd be funny. But instead, Mick reached for her hand, took it in his and said softly, "I wouldn't embarrass you, Carrie. Please know that."

Carrie nodded and soon began to settle down, but Mick held on to her hand even after she stopped trembling.

Paul, the garda, was acting emcee, a role he took seriously every year. When he announced them and asked them to join him onstage, Mick gave Carrie's hand a quick squeeze before they walked out together.

"Couple number three is an example of a US–Irish relationship at its best. She's a journalist from Philly. He's a matchmaker who just might have met his match. Can they get their love on the front page before it becomes old news? Let's welcome Mick Foley and Carrie Fields!"

The stage lights were blinding, and even though he couldn't see the audience, Mick knew the community center was packed. It always was for this event.

As they sat down next to each other at a table placed in the middle of the stage, Paul paced the stage and spoke into the microphone. "This is a simple game of truth and dare." Paul held up his right hand and indicated that Mick and Carrie should do the same.

Carrie looked at Mick nervously and followed his lead, raising her right hand.

Paul said, "Repeat after me: I do solemnly swear by the holy vow of matrimony and the love that makes the world go around that I will tell the truth and nothing but the truth when asked and complete the dare I'm given to the best of my ability."

Mick and Carrie mumbled the oath together.

"Here's how this works: you'll each be given one truth and one dare. Ladies first," Paul said, spinning on his heel with his microphone in his hand. Turning to Carrie he said, "Ready?"

Carrie nodded.

"How old were you when you had your first kiss, and can you tell us about it?"

Carrie giggled and Mick felt her relax beside him. Carrie cleared her throat and announced, "I was five when I had my first kiss."

"Five!" Paul feigned astonishment. "Mick, did you know Miss Fields had wanton ways?"

Mick laughed. "No, I did not."

"Tell us the story, Carrie, we're all on the edge of our seats," Paul said.

"I was in the cloakroom at school, and Joey Melita was there putting his coat on and well, I just kissed him!"

"Are you always that impulsive?" Paul asked.

"Unfortunately, yes."

"You better watch her, Mick, she's a live one."

Mick looked over at her longingly and said, "Oh, I've got my eye on her."

"All right, Mick, it's your turn. "Have you ever been in love?"

"Just once," Mick replied.

"Really?" Paul could not hide his surprise. "Was she the one who got away?"

Mick smiled but revealed nothing. It remained to be seen.

Paul turned to the audience and said, "Our resident matchmaker is a sandbagger. Who knew?"

A wave of *aws* twittered through the audience. Mick stole a glance at Carrie. She regarded him with an unreadable expression. He smiled and winked at her, and she rewarded him with a smile.

"Now, are you ready for your dares?" Paul asked. "Mick, you'll go first in this round. Are you ready for your dare?"

"I am," Mick said good-naturedly. He was enjoying himself and he hoped Carrie was too. She had relaxed quite a bit since backstage.

"Mick Foley, I dare you to complete a limerick about Carrie. I can give you five or ten minutes to think of one. But please, for the sake of our audience, keep it clean," Paul said.

Carrie looked at him, her eyes bright. He winked at her and shifted in his chair, leaning forward to look at the stage floor as he thought. He knew the rhyming pattern of a limerick. It was five-verse poem with an AABBA rhyme scheme.

Finally, he lifted his head and said into the microphone in front of him:

"There once was a girl from the U, S of A
Who arrived in Kilcornan just before May.
Pretty was she,
And if it was up to me,
I'd kiss her all through the long day."

The audience erupted in shouts and clapping. Mick smiled and looked over at Carrie, who was blushing.

"Now, Carrie, are you ready for your dare?" Paul asked.

"I hope so," she said nervously.

"Your dare is you have to sing a song for Mick," Paul said.

Mick raised his eyebrows, thinking this should be interesting.

"I can't sing!" Carrie protested.

Paul said, "It doesn't matter. You're among friends."

Mick gave her an encouraging smile, hoping it would help calm her nerves. He had to admit she'd been a good sport with all of it.

"Would you step up to the mic, Miss Fields," Paul instructed.

Carrie looked as if she wanted to bolt. Mick noticed she was shaking, and he was just about to stand up and put a halt to it when Carrie stood and walked over to the mic, fidgeting with her hands.

"All right, Miss Fields, you can either sing or recite it as a poem, and just one verse will do," Paul instructed. "If you choose to sing, it will have to be a capella as there is no musical accompaniment."

Carrie nodded and pushed her bangs out of her eyes.

Paul placed the mic in the stand and adjusted it for her height. He turned the mic a bit so she would not have her back to Mick, nor would she have to face the audience directly.

Mick sat forward, curious, wondering what she would sing.

Carrie coughed and cleared her throat. She began, her voice low and barely audible, and then she increased her volume slightly. She wobbled a bit in the beginning but soon controlled the tremor in her voice. She closed her eyes and looked as if she were dreaming.

As soon she sang the first line, Mick recognized the song. He straightened up in his chair and swallowed hard. He was stunned. "She Moved through the Fair" had been a song he'd introduced her to those few weeks they had together after they were married. It had been on one of his CDs. They'd listened to it as they drove all over Boston together, as they played cards, or as they drank a cup of tea. At the time, it had been his favorite song, but it had reminded him so much of Carrie that he hadn't listened to it since then.

Mick didn't take his eyes off of her. Emotion and feelings that threatened to pull him under and out to sea quickly overwhelmed him. He realized he was still in love with Carrie. He'd never stopped loving her.

Carrie's voice cracked in a few places. It wasn't perfect, but it was beautiful. When she opened her eyes, she looked at Mick and smiled.

The audience broke into cheers and claps. Mick bolted out of his seat, carried by a current of emotion, and gathered her up in his arms and pulled her close to him, not missing the look of surprise on her face. He held her close, delighting in her arms sliding around his waist.

The moment was perfect.

Chapter Fifteen

A FTER THE TRUTH AND Dare contest, Carrie walked hand in hand with Mick down the main street of Kilcornan, feeling content. There hadn't been much conversation, each happy to bask in the glow of the moment. Him holding her hand as they strolled along felt natural, like their hands were meant for each other. People waved to them as they walked by, and it gave Carrie a sense of belonging. When other people or couples stopped to talk to them, Mick immediately introduced her: "This is Carrie," or "Have you met Carrie?" And he'd give her hand a little reassuring squeeze. Everyone was delighted for Mick and made comments like, "It's about time!" or "Finally! A match for the matchmaker." Some of the men slapped him on the back and laughed. "Welcome to the club!" Everyone she met was welcoming and lovely.

As they walked along, Mick pointed out things of interest to her and told her bits of history about the town. They found themselves standing in front of the empty, dusty windows of the old newspaper's office. Carrie peered in like she always did, thinking it was a shame that the town had lost its paper.

"What happened here?" she asked. They had stopped walking. Mick had not let go of her hand, and she had not let go of his, either.

"This was the town's newspaper," Mick explained. "The owner died unexpectedly, and his only child lives in England and has no interest in returning to Kilcornan to run it. It's kind of sad, really, because it was a little town paper that kept everyone connected. But there doesn't seem to be anyone who wants to take it up."

"So it's for sale?" she asked.

"It is," Mick said. "Everything is still there for printing. Even the old receptionist, Helen, is still around here in Kilcornan. Losing the newspaper was a great loss."

"I bet," Carrie agreed. Newspapers were so important.

They stood there, looking in at the abandoned office, holding hands. Carrie felt happy, something she hadn't felt in a long time.

"Don't look now, but Charlotte Connors is walking up the street," Mick whispered.

Carrie stayed still, not turning her head or even talking.

"Will you let me kiss you, so she'll keep walking and not pester us? It's been such a great evening, I don't want her to ruin it," Mick said, looking past Carrie at the approaching interloper.

Carrie didn't know how she felt about that, but she found herself nodding as her voice came out in a squeak. "Yeah, sure."

Mick smiled down at her. He placed his hands on either side of her face. Carrie held her breath and didn't take her eyes off his. Her heartbeat raged inside of her. The sound was deafening in her ears.

"Your skin is so soft," Mick murmured. He looked mesmerized, as if he had lost focus.

As Mick leaned toward her, Carrie's lips parted in expectation. Her heart banged against her chest. She slid her arms around his waist, leaning against him for support, as her knees felt wobbly. His lips pressed against hers. He kissed her softly at first, almost with hesitation, like dipping one's foot into a cool stream. Carrie yielded to him. She liked the way it felt to be in his arms. Liked how he kissed her. Carrie soon forgot everything: why she was in Ireland, the reason they were kissing, and even her name. Gradually, his hands left her face as he pulled her closer to him in a warm embrace. They kissed a bit more until suddenly, Mick pulled away from her, leaving her breathless and disoriented.

Wow! Now that was a kiss. She stole a glance at Mick, wondering if the kiss had affected him the way it had affected her. He gave her a quick smile, shoved his hands in his pockets and said, "Let's walk on. We can check on some of the dancing and the pubs."

He stepped back out onto the road, leaving Carrie no choice but to follow him. He didn't even hold her hand. Was she that horrible of a kisser? Granted it had caught her by surprise, but she did go with it. She didn't say anything. Disappointment crushed her. He'd only kissed her to keep Charlotte away. And somehow, this depressed her.

Carrie had just climbed into bed when Kathy arrived in the room, her hair a mess, her cheeks flushed, and her makeup faded.

Carrie sat up. "And where have you been all day?" she teased.

Kathy sat on her bed across from Carrie's, unbelted her jacket, slid it off, and tossed it on a chair across the room. It hit the chair and slid to the floor. Kathy shrugged. "Where haven't I been today? I haven't been back here since I left this morning."

Carrie raised an eyebrow and scooted back until she was leaning against the headboard. She tucked a pillow behind her. "Where'd you go?" she asked, curious.

"Would you believe it if I told you Ronan drove me to County Carlow? He wanted to show me his farm!"

"No way!" Carrie laughed.

"Yes way. He even took me for a ride in his tractor," Kathy said.

"You seem to be enjoying his company," Carrie noted.

"I am, but he knows I'm not looking for anything, not even a fling," Kathy said. "I've spent five years with David, and just because we're taking a break doesn't give me the right to cheat on him."

Carrie nodded.

"I told Ronan that I won't be seeing him anymore," Kathy said. "I just can't."

"How did he take it?" Carrie asked.

Kathy smiled. "He was Ronan. He was kind and understanding." She inhaled a deep breath. "But the truth is, he's just not David."

Carrie waited. She knew her friend wanted to talk. It was not up to her to praise or criticize David. It was her job as Kathy's best friend just to listen. And although she did like David, it wasn't her place to push Kathy in either direction. Carrie knew David well, and she still believed that David loved Kathy. But Kathy had to come to that conclusion herself or make the decision to move on without him.

"Maybe I've been with David for too long," Kathy said. Carrie thought her friend looked tired, and realized that the separation, the drama, the change of scenery might be taking their toll on her.

"How so?"

"David makes me laugh." Kathy sighed. "I'm used to David entertaining me with his funny, sarcastic running commentary."

"Isn't Ronan funny?" Carrie asked. Not everyone had a sense of humor.

"His humor is cornier, you know, like Dad jokes?" Kathy said.

Carrie winced. "Oh boy."

"And David always opens the door for me or lets me go first into a place," Kathy said.

"And Ronan doesn't?"

Kathy shook her head. "Nope. It's every man for himself." Carrie picked up a tiny hint of exasperation and resisted laughing. The bloom was fading off the new rose. Kathy picked at imaginary lint on the duvet cover. She stared at it. "It's not his fault; Ronan is a super-nice guy." She shrugged and looked over at Carrie, her eyes filled with tears.

Carrie jumped out of her bed, sat next to her friend, and put her arm around Kathy as her body shook with wracking sobs.

"Hey, hey, what's this about?" Carrie asked, concerned.

"And David calls me 'Babe' and I miss that," Kathy wailed.

Carrie rubbed her back and laughed. "You like him calling you that?"

Between sobs, Kathy said with a laugh, "I know it's cheesy but that's our thing."

Carrie didn't want to know what nickname Kathy had for David. But still, she thought it was nice that their relationship, even though it was a little rocky, had had some good and tender moments.

Kathy pulled a tissue from her pocket and wiped her eyes. Once Kathy settled down, Carrie asked, "Do you want to go home?"

Kathy shook her head. "No, not really. Even if I went home to him, we'd still have problems."

"If you love him and you think he's the one for you long-term, then you'll figure out a way to make it work," Carrie told her.

Kathy gave her a quick smile. "Thanks for listening, Carrie. You're such a good friend."

She leaned in and hugged Carrie.

Chapter Sixteen

MICK THOUGHT ABOUT THAT kiss. That one kiss had occupied every waking moment since it had happened. Her lips had been so warm and yielding, and she had been so eager. When he'd started to get lost in it, he got scared. Terrified. The kiss was wonderful. Afterward, he couldn't so much as hold her hand. Not because he didn't want to. But because he didn't trust himself not to touch her again.

And Carrie had gone quiet on him. Either he had overstepped his bounds and she'd been offended by the kiss. Or maybe—just maybe—it had affected her the same way it had affected him. But he was too afraid to ask. Afraid that it might be the former and not the latter.

Quietly, they'd gone on to the pubs. He bought them drinks. Their conversation had been general, like the kind you'd have with a stranger next to you on the bus. Nothing too deep. No banter, no joking. When they were in the dance halls, he didn't ask her to dance. He couldn't. To have her in his arms again would be his undoing. As much as he wanted to, he resisted. He didn't trust himself.

At the end of the evening, he'd walked her back to the Caherdavin Arms. Foregoing any attempts at any more stilted or forced conversation, they walked in silence. But even the silence was charged, as if a sudden loud noise or movement would cause an explosion.

Carrie had spoken first, breaking the deafening silence. "I was hoping we could have one more sit-down so I can tie up some loose ends for my assignment."

Mick tried not to be irritated about the fact that the only thing she seemed interested in was her newspaper article.

"How about tomorrow night? You can come over to my place," he said, studying her reaction. He added quickly, "That's if you don't mind."

Carrie chuckled. "You know, Mick, I don't even know where you live!"

He smiled at her. "I live in a flat above the café. There's a door right next to the café entrance."

Carrie rubbed her arms and he wondered if she was cold. "What time?"

"Is eight all right or is that too late?"

"That's perfect."

They had arrived in front of the Caherdavin Arms and there was nothing more to say. Mick studied Carrie under the illumination of the streetlights. She looked tired. There were purple circles under her eyes. He resisted reaching out and touching her face, balling his fists in his pockets. Before he could do something stupid, like kiss her again, he said, "Well, goodnight, Carrie. I'll see you tomorrow."

"Goodnight, Mick," she said softly, and she turned and hurried up the path to the door of the hotel. Not once did she look back over her shoulder at him. When she was safely inside the hotel, Mick had headed back toward home.

Not quite ready to call it a night, Mick decided to stretch his legs. He strolled toward the end of town with no particular destination in mind, engaging in conversations along the way with whomever he met.

He spotted Marie on the other side of the street. He was disappointed to see her alone and couldn't help but wonder where her husband was. She walked with her head down. He knew that look all too well; there was nothing worse than being at a festival that celebrated love and romance when your own relationship was rocky.

He called out to her. "Marie!"

She looked up when she heard her name and smiled when she recognized him.

He crossed the road to meet her. "How are you? Are you enjoying yourself?"

"Oh, yeah, I love coming here, the memories," she said.

But Mick felt she wasn't telling the truth. He had the impression she was putting on a brave front. He had loads of sympathy for her. She just looked so sad.

"Where's Jim?"

Marie looked around and said vaguely, "I don't know. He's probably in one of the pubs having a pint."

Marie was a sound woman. Any man would be lucky to have her. She had a husband who didn't appreciate her, and that made Mick angry.

"Will you walk with me and keep me company?" he asked.

She nodded. "Sure, I can do that."

Mick asked her what she did back in County Meath.

"I'm a receptionist for a bread maker," she said. "I know it's nothing fancy."

He stopped in his tracks. He wasn't having it, this woman putting herself down.

"Do you like your job?"

Marie smiled. "I do. The other girls I work with in the office are really lovely. And once a week, the owner gives us free bread and faery cakes and stuff, which my boys love," she said with a laugh.

"Don't ever apologize for doing something you love," Mick advised. "No matter what it is." It was a lesson he had had to learn himself over the years.

She nodded and they kept on walking.

"You have three children, correct?" Mick asked.

She smiled. "You have a good memory. Yes, three boys. They're good lads."

"How old are they?"

"Nine, seven, and five."

"And what does Jim do?" he asked.

"Jim works for the County Council," she answered proudly.

They'd just passed Dirty Bertie's when the pub door opened and music spilled out, along with Marie's husband, Jim.

Jim staggered out, smiling and laughing, but his merriment disappeared when he spied his wife. Mick saw red. Jim reminded him too much of his own father for Mick to cut him any slack.

"What are you doing? Following me?" Jim sneered at his wife.

Marie looked shocked and hurt.

Mick looked at him, surprised. "She was walking with me."

Jim turned on him. "I didn't ask you. I'm talking to my wife."

Marie spoke softly. "It's okay, Mick. Thanks anyway."

Mick politely walked away, practically biting off his tongue, knowing he shouldn't interfere. As he did, he heard Jim raise his voice to Marie.

If there was one thing Mick couldn't stand, it was a woman being bullied. He had seen enough of that growing up, in the way his father had mistreated his mother.

"Hey, Jim, I hope you're not using that tone of voice talking to your wife," Mick challenged. He saw the look on Marie's face and hoped his interference wouldn't cause trouble for her later.

Jim spun around to face him. "What concern is it of yours?"

"Whenever a woman is being mistreated, it is always my concern," Mick said with a clipped voice.

"Please," Jim said in a mocking tone.

"It's okay, Mick, I can handle him," Marie said quietly.

"Handle me?" Jim roared. "What am I, a dog?"

"No, I didn't mean it like that," Marie stammered. "It's just I've grown used to your behavior."

Mick assessed the situation and said pointedly, "Marie, I am so very sorry that I didn't meet you before you met Jim. I would have found you a partner that was worthy and deserving of you."

Marie stared at him open-mouthed.

Enraged, Jim swung at him, sputtering, "Why you—"

But Mick managed to catch his arm and deflect the punch.

"Mick, what's going on?" came the voice of Paul, the local garda. He charged toward them.

"Jim, now look what you've done!" Marie hissed.

"Don't tell me what I've done!" Jim bellowed.

"Hey, hey," Paul warned. "Lower your voice. We don't go taking swings at people here. Now straighten yourself up or I'll have to put some manners on you."

Jim grumbled something incoherent.

"Is he harassing you?" Paul asked Marie.

"I'm his wife."

"Condolences," Paul said.

Marie laughed. It was the first time Mick had seen her do so.

"It wasn't that funny, Marie," Jim said. He turned to the garda. "We're fine." He grabbed Marie by the arm and said, "Come on, let's go."

Mick and Paul didn't take their eyes off the couple as they walked away.

"That poor woman," Paul said.

Mick couldn't have said it better himself.

Mick did a quick tidy-up of his flat before Carrie arrived. He kept the lighting soft and minimal, deciding on just two tabletop lamps. He made up a plate of cheese and crackers.

Carrie was punctual. She wore a navy maxi dress with a cardigan. A grouping of bracelets jangled on her wrist. She looked beautiful. When she stepped into his living space, she looked around nervously, and he wondered what it looked like through her eyes.

He didn't have a lot, but his furniture was comfortable. There was a sofa, an easy chair, and a coffee table sitting on top of a small area rug. There was a television in the corner that he rarely watched and some copies of artwork on the walls. But it was all the books that made it home. Shelves lined two walls and they were packed with books, mostly non-fiction historical tomes and some fiction, mainly thrillers. Next to the easy chair was an end table, and on top of that were two books he was currently reading. The flat was open plan, with a kitchen at the back of the sitting area with glossy white contemporary cabinets and black appliances. It might not be much, but it was home. He liked it.

"Nice place," Carrie concluded. She looked at everything but him.

"Please, sit down," he said, indicating the sofa. Carrie chose the easy chair and pulled out a notebook and pen from her purse before setting it down on the floor next to a pile of books.

"Would you like some wine? Or something else? A cup of tea?" he asked.

Carrie shook her head. "No thanks."

"If you change your mind, just let me know," he instructed.

"You'll be the first," she said with a tight smile.

"Do you mind if I have something?" he asked.

"No, of course not, make yourself at home," she said.

He laughed; she was adorable. She blushed and muttered, "Well you are at home, so you don't have to make yourself at home." She blew out a breath of air that lifted her bangs from her forehead. "Never mind."

Mick went back to the kitchen and skipped the tea and just poured himself a glass of water instead. He returned and laid the cheese platter on the coffee table. He helped himself to an olive and a piece of cheese, popping both into his mouth at the same time. He settled into a corner of the sofa.

"Okay, I'm ready for the interview," he said, trying for casual to put her at ease and get her to smile. He wanted to make it right between them but wasn't sure how to do that.

Carrie opened her notebook and uncapped her pen. "Just some final questions so I can tie this all together."

"Ask away," he said.

Jumping right in, she asked, "When did you first realize you had the gift for matchmaking? How old were you?" She was cute when she was serious.

Mick looked up to the ceiling, trying to remember. "It wasn't like I had a moment of awareness about having the gift that my mother and grandmother had, but I'd say it started in secondary school. One of my mates, Kevin, had this girlfriend that was just no good for him. And he was miserable. Kept trying to figure out how to make it work. And I was like, 'Man, you're trying too hard. We're only seventeen!' I suggested that another girl in our class, this girl named Susan, would be much more suited to him. We went back and forth like this for about six months before he finally broke up with this other girl and took Susan out."

Carrie scribbled furiously in shorthand in her notebook. "And how did that work out?"

Mick shrugged. "It must have worked out all right, because they're still together. And that's almost twenty years."

"Hmm," she said thoughtfully as she tapped her pen against her bottom lip.

Mick sipped his water, waiting for the next question.

Carrie regarded him for a moment. "I remember you used to want to be a history teacher. Secondary school."

He was touched that she remembered.

"But you're not a history teacher, you're a matchmaker. What happened?"

He shrugged, setting down his glass. "I hadn't planned on it, but when my mother died, I took over."

"Your sister couldn't take over as the matchmaker?"

Mick laughed at the thought of Rosemary as a matchmaker. "No, she doesn't possess the gift. I took over the running of the festival that first year, and I guess because it was always the matchmaker who'd been in charge of it, people just started coming to me for relationship advice. And then gradually, I started making matches. By the time the second festival rolled around after my mother's death, I was in the full swing of things." He almost added, "And I never looked back." But he didn't want to hurt her feelings.

He stood up, needing to stretch his legs and move around. "Are you sure you don't want anything to drink?"

Without looking up at him, she said, "Positive, thanks."

He was at a loss for words.

"You're practically a celebrity," she observed.

"Only in Kilcornan," he joked. Carrie gave him a polite smile.

"Do you like being a matchmaker?"

Mick didn't hesitate. "I do. It's not like work at all. Every day I get up and go to a job that I love. It's all about helping people find their happiness with another person."

"What does the future hold for you as a matchmaker?" she asked.

Mick appeared thoughtful. "Traditional matchmaking is just as relevant today as it was a hundred years ago. More than ever, in fact."

"How so?"

"The festival is a lot of fun," he said. "But it's more than that. There's an unspoken understanding that despite all the fun and the dancing, you're there to meet someone, hopefully a lifetime partner. It's the difference between going into a shop and online shopping. You go into a store, you browse, and you make your selection. But you order something online and you can't really be sure of what you're getting until you see it. Will I like it? Will it fit?"

Carrie asked a few more questions. More than once, he wished he was brave enough to break the ice.

"Well, thanks for your time," Carrie said, jumping up from the chair. She threw her pen into her purse, then folded her notebook closed and tucked it into the side pocket.

"Is that it? Don't you want to ask more questions?" he asked, not wanting her to leave. She had hardly looked at him during the evening. Mick stood up from the sofa.

"Do you want me to?" she asked.

"I mean, you don't have to go if you don't want to," he said, realizing how desperate he sounded.

"It's getting late," she said. It wasn't even ten.

Mick followed her to the door.

She tried opening the door, but the deadbolt was on. She spun it one way and then the other, but the lock remained engaged. "I can't seem to get this door open." She laughed, but her laugh sounded shrill and full of frustration.

"Let me, it can be a bit tricky," he said. Up close and personal and right behind her, he breathed in the scent of her. He didn't want her to go. He wanted her to stay. He reached past her shoulder and turned the deadbolt, and the door sprung open. He laid a hand on her shoulder and whispered, "Carrie."

But she slipped out from under his arm and gave him a tight smile. "Well, goodnight, Mick, I'll see you around." And she was gone, her footsteps echoing down the staircase, slamming the door behind her.

Mick banged his hand against the door in frustration. He didn't know what he had done to make her so upset.

Mick plopped down on the sofa and ran a hand through his hair. He glanced at the cheese platter. The olives were starting to look withered and forlorn, and the cheese was getting sweaty. He gave it a miss.

He reviewed things in his mind. Everything had been fine up until that kiss. Because afterwards, he had backed off. He sighed, upset with himself. That's why she was upset. It had to be. He kept sending her mixed signals. She probably didn't know whether she was coming or going. But how to make it right, that was the question.

Chapter Seventeen

Carrie rushed out onto the street from Mick's apartment and drew in a lungful of the cool night air. Her face burned. Had his apartment been that hot, or had the whole interview been that awkward and uncomfortable? How could they possibly continue like this, pretending nothing ever happened between them all those years ago? And that kiss the day before? What did it mean? Had they just been caught up in the moment? Had it meant nothing to him at all?

Carrie straightened up and drew in another breath. Over the tops of the buildings across the way, the night sky was inky with a glittering expanse of stars.

Charlotte Connors stepped into Carrie's path, startling her.

"Oh, Charlotte, you scared me," Carrie said with a nervous laugh. The Caherdavin Arms was in her sight, and that meant she wasn't far away from her bed and the end of this day.

But Charlotte didn't smile. "I saw you just left Mick's."

"I did. I had to finish my interview with him for my newspaper," Carrie answered.

Charlotte scoffed. "Do I look stupid to you?"

Carrie frowned at her in confusion.

"You just waltz into our town and take over," Charlotte hissed. "I told you that Mick and I were developing feelings for one another. And what did you do? You went after him yourself. So much for women empowering each other!"

"I—"

Charlotte cut her off. "You have gone out of your way to steal him from me. The cook-off. The race. And then the Truth and Dare." Charlotte narrowed her eyes. "All of this was some part of a deliberate scheme on your part to steal Mick from me."

Carrie didn't have the heart to tell her that Mick belonged to no one.

"Look, Charlotte, I had nothing to do with those events. Other people signed us up." She realized how lame it sounded.

"Here's the thing, Carrie. You're an outsider. You'll always be an outsider. You will never fit in here in Kilcornan, no matter how much you try," Charlotte said.

Carrie's face burned as if she'd been slapped. "Step aside, Charlotte," she commanded. Charlotte stepped aside. Carrie ran to her hotel, fed up with Mick, with Charlotte, and most of all this festival where love and romance were king.

"Go back to your charmed life in the States!" Charlotte called out after her.

Once she was safely inside the lobby, Carrie leaned against the wall, realizing she'd been holding her breath the entire way. She stopped on her way to the staircase to pet the dog, who was in his usual position: sound asleep on the ottoman in front of a dying fire.

Kathy sat on her bed in her pajamas, filing her nails. She smiled when Carrie walked through the door.

"Hello, stranger," she said. "How've you been?"

Carrie dropped down to the edge of her bed and threw her purse aside.

Kathy's smile disappeared. "What's wrong? You don't look right. Has something happened?"

That was all the opening Carrie needed. She rolled her eyes. "What hasn't happened?" She relayed the incident with Charlotte. Carrie bit her lip. Tears threatened.

"The nerve of her!" Kathy scowled.

"She said I went after Mick," Carrie repeated, still feeling wounded.

"What business is it of hers?" Kathy protested.

Carrie shrugged.

Kathy's face relaxed. "You should have told her you're married to him!"

With this statement, the tears burst forth from Carrie. Kathy looked on in horror.

"What is it? What's wrong?" Kathy asked.

Carrie took a deep breath and poured forth her story about the kiss.

"It's about time!" Kathy clapped after Carrie told her about the kiss.

Noticing Carrie's facial expression, Kathy asked, "Oh no, what happened?" She set down the nail file on the bedside table located between their beds.

"He's been acting funny since he kissed me. Strange, like," Carrie blurted out. "I mean, was I that bad of a kisser? I get the impression that he's sorry he did it, you know? Like he's regretting everything."

Kathy looked at her. "Have you asked him? Talked about this kiss?"

Carrie shook her head.

"You ask questions and investigate things for a living, and you won't ask Mick Foley the most important questions you could ever ask?" Kathy looked over at her in disbelief.

"How do I bring that up?" Carrie asked. "Do I just go in there and say, 'Am I good kisser or what?'"

Kathy laughed. "No, of course not. You could feel him out."

"How?"

Kathy shrugged. "Maybe you could ask him, 'Can we talk about that kiss?'"

Carrie made a dismissive gesture.

"What?" Kathy asked. "What's the alternative? Moping around for the rest of the vacation, speculating as to how he feels about you? Trying to guess and then possibly arriving at the wrong conclusion?" Kathy paused before adding, "Carrie, you have a right to know what's going on with your own marriage."

When Carrie didn't say anything, Kathy added, "If that kiss meant that much to you, if it affected you that much, then there's a strong possibility it affected him, as well."

Carrie made a face. She knew she could ask him those questions, and if she weren't emotionally invested, she would have. But the possibility that he might give her an answer she wouldn't like prevented her from doing so.

"I'll have to figure something out," Carrie said. She then asked, "How are things going with you?"

Kathy rolled her eyes. "Ugh. I sent David a text today."

"Oh no."

"I realize now that I shouldn't have."

"But you couldn't stand the fact that you haven't heard from him," Carrie said with a knowing smile.

"Yeah, something like that," Kathy agreed. "He texted back, 'I'm fine.'"

"And?" Carrie asked, not comprehending.

"He's fine? That's it? No, 'How are you? When are you coming home? I miss you'?" she raised her voice on the last question.

"You're supposed to be taking a break."

"Yeah, but I don't want him enjoying himself too much while I'm gone!"

"When we get home, will you please sit down and have an honest conversation with him? You expect him to read your mind, and that's not fair."

"Maybe. I don't know," Kathy said sourly.

"Go to sleep, and we'll be home soon, and you can work on it then," Carrie said.

Kathy turned the bedside light off, and Carrie decided she'd run a hot bath and then look over her notes and work on the rough draft of her article.

After her bath, wrapped up in her big, fluffy robe, she tiptoed back to her bed so as not to wake her friend. She leaned back against the headboard, stretched out her legs, and opened her laptop.

The following morning, Carrie and Kathy left Kilcornan for the day to do some sightseeing. It had been Kathy's suggestion, and Carrie had jumped at the chance. As much as she'd grown to love Kilcornan, she needed to put some distance between her and Mick.

The hotel had a stand for brochures and day trips located in the lobby, not too far from the sleeping dog. In the end, after perusing a handful of brochures, they narrowed their choices down to either a day trip via boat to the Aran Islands or a bus tour of the Ring of Kerry.

They chose the day trip out to the Aran Islands, located off the west coast, near Galway.

The day was overcast for the first time since they'd arrived, so they took their rain jackets and umbrellas with them. They finally got to see all the rain everyone talked about in relation to Ireland.

As the boat headed out to the islands, Carrie stared back at the mainland, thinking of Mick. But her attention was diverted by the constant rocking of the boat on the choppy waters. By the time they pulled in to the largest of the Aran Islands, Inis Mor, both Carrie and Kathy were hanging over the side of the boat, eyes bloodshot and faces splotchy from vomiting.

After the boat was secured to the dock, they were helped off, and they staggered arm in arm up the pier, grateful to be on terra firma again. The rain had stopped and had been replaced by intermittent sun and a fresh breeze with a salty mist. Once their equilibrium stabilized, they rented a couple of bikes and set off to cycle around the island.

The island itself was a mass of gray rock—limestone, they were told—with patches of grass. Across the open island there appeared to be a grid of low stone walls. Wind from off the Atlantic blew across the island and buffeted them.

Several times they stopped and got off their bikes to rest against a stone wall and eat some of the candy bars Kathy had stuffed in her pockets. Despite the wind whipping their hair around their faces, they enjoyed the views of the Atlantic and the mainland.

It went well until Carrie's bike hit a depression in the narrow road and she went off course. A low stone wall unceremoniously brought her to a rough stop, dumping her off her bike, but other than a grazed knee, she was unhurt.

They decided that that was enough, and it was time for a meal.

They landed at a little whitewashed cottage that had been converted into a small café. They went inside and ordered their meals and some coffee, their faces damp from the mist and red from exertion.

Over their meal, they commiserated over Mick and David.

"You know what our problem is?" Kathy asked, buttering a slice of brown bread. "We're too nice."

Was that it? Somehow, Carrie doubted it.

"It's David I want," Kathy said.

"Are you sure?" Carrie asked.

Kathy nodded. "You know what? We need to fight for what we want!"

Carrie cut into her meal and slid a forkful of pot roast into her mouth. "What do you mean?"

"We need to lay everything out on the table," Kathy said, picking up her salad fork and waving it around in the air. "Enough waiting for them to make the first move." Kathy's eyes grew bright, and a smile emerged. "When I go home, I'm going to tell David exactly how I feel, and then I'm going to ask him to marry me!"

Carrie's fork paused midair. "I think you're right. It's time to have an honest conversation with David."

"And I suggest you do the same with Mick before we leave," Kathy said.

Carrie hesitated. "Oh, I don't know. I already asked him to marry me once. That hasn't worked out so well."

Kathy pressed her lips together. "You know what I mean. Why wouldn't you?"

"Because I don't know if I could bear the final rejection," Carrie said.

"I'm going to put on my mom hat and give you a little bit of tough love. You need to move on with your life, either way. With or without Mick. You've been in a holding pattern for more than ten years, the best years of your life!" Kathy paused and took a sip of her water. "It might be painful. But then you can get a divorce and move on with your life."

Carrie didn't know if she wanted to move on with her life without Mick.

"Or maybe he just needs a shove, like David," Kathy said.

Carrie sighed. "I don't know if I want someone who needs a shove to love me. To be with me. I'd like him to come up with the idea all by himself."

It was true; she was tired of waiting. And maybe she was chasing after a dream that had stalled her personal life. Maybe it was time to get a divorce and put the dream of Mick to rest once and for all.

Kathy was saying something.

"Sorry, what did you say?" Carrie asked.

"I said, do you want me to talk to him on your behalf? I'm happy to do it," Kathy said. "I'd like to give him a piece of my mind."

"No, please don't do that," Carrie pleaded. "I'll talk to him. And get it over with."

"Don't be so negative. Maybe he does love you."

Carrie tilted her head to one side and scoffed at that idea. "If that was true, you'd think he would have told me by now."

They decided dessert was called for, and once finished they headed off to catch the ferry back to the mainland, both dreading the boat ride and finding it funny at the same time.

When they reached the pier, Carrie plopped down on the low brick wall that surrounded the parking lot as they waited for the boat. The view was breathtaking.

Chapter Eighteen

MICK STROLLED THROUGH THE cemetery. It was the only place in town that was quiet, because as the festival neared its conclusion, the crowd was getting louder and rowdier. It was as if they were trying to pack every last ounce of their collective energy into the final hours. A slight drizzle had started, but he'd left his umbrella back at home and he had no intention of going back for it.

Carrie would be leaving soon, and he supposed they should have a chat. He was going to offer to divorce her. He'd lain awake all night thinking about her and had concluded that there was no way it could work between them. He'd complicated her life, and he wasn't going to keep on holding her back.

His home and life were here in Kilcornan. Going to America when he was younger had been fine. And almost expected. But now he was too deeply rooted in his hometown and his legacy as the town's matchmaker. He couldn't expect Carrie to give up her life and family to join him here. And he wouldn't dream of asking her. Plus, she had a successful career as a journalist. There wasn't even a newspaper in Kilcornan anymore.

He also believed she'd be better off without him. Memories of how his father treated his mother haunted him. He couldn't bear it if he turned out like him: indifferent to those who loved him. And although Mick didn't drink, he'd proven that he had a fear of expressing how he felt and seeing his commitments through. Just like his father.

The obstacles were insurmountable.

"Hello, Mick!" Charlotte called.

Mick grimaced, squeezing his eyes shut. He couldn't help but wonder if Charlotte had put a tracking device on him, as it always seemed to him that she managed to locate him no matter where he went. With a heavy sigh, he turned around to face her. It was also time to deal with this situation once and for all.

"Charlotte, good morning," he said, managing a smile.

"Good morning," she enthused. She wore a green mackintosh with red apples on it over a red corduroy skirt and green shoes. "What happened to our beautiful weather?"

Mick gazed up at the dull sky. The cloud cover was heavy. It certainly matched his mood. Hopefully, it would clear soon.

"I'm glad I caught up with you," Charlotte said.

Mick knew it was no coincidence she'd run into him. Knowing Charlotte, she'd probably been all over town looking for him.

"Why?"

"We need to talk about that American," Charlotte said with a roll of her eyes.

"Which one?" Mick asked.

"The journalist. I know she's been pestering you," Charlotte said.

"Carrie Fields?"

"I've seen the way she's been throwing herself at you since she arrived. She's as bold as brass, that one." Charlotte smirked. "It's shameful really. I'm embarrassed for her."

"Carrie hasn't been throwing herself at me," Mick objected.

"Oh, come on, Mick, you must have seen the way she looks at you," Charlotte said.

Had he missed something?

"And her manipulation of the couples' activities just so she could be with you is downright awful," she said.

Mick didn't bother reminding Charlotte that she herself had tried to coordinate things so she could be Mick's partner.

"Be careful, those types can be dangerous," she said. "Stalkers."

Mick looked directly at Charlotte. "I know all about that."

"Good. I told her exactly what I thought of her."

Mick frowned. "What do you mean?"

"I told her her behavior was shameful."

"You didn't!"

"I most certainly did," Charlotte said.

Mick lowered his head and tried not to lose his temper. This was all his fault. He couldn't blame Charlotte.

"I wish you wouldn't have done that," he said.

"Why not?"

"Because I'm in love with Carrie Fields and have been for a very long time," he said.

Charlotte's mouth fell open and stayed open. Eventually, she recovered and said, "Are you serious?"

"I am."

"Why didn't you tell me? Why did you lead me to believe there was something between us?"

"No, Charlotte, I've never led you on. I've tried to tell you. I'm telling you now. There is nothing between us and there never will be." To soften the blow, he added, "There is someone out there for you, trust me. Will I try to find a match for you?" It would be a challenge, that was for sure.

"Oh no, I don't believe in that stuff! I'd rather pick my own mate, thanks very much." She appeared thoughtful and then asked him, "Does this mean I can't come back to Kilcornan anymore?"

⁓ ℓℓℓ ⁓

Mick spotted Carrie and Kathy exiting a cab in front of the Caherdavin Arms in the evening. He called out to Carrie. She hesitated, said something to Kathy, and finally walked toward him.

"Do you have a minute?" he asked.

"Sure," she said. She looked back at Kathy and waved her on.

"Will we walk on?" he asked, with a nod toward the town center.

He intended to find a secluded spot somewhere in the park. He dreaded the conversation that they had to have. But it was best to get it over with.

But they only got as far as the narrow stone bridge that arched over the River Cora.

Carrie leaned over its edge and looked down at the water coursing over a riverbed full of rocks.

"It's so pretty here," she said.

"It's called the Bridge of Tears," Mick told her.

Carrie looked up at him, curious. "Why do they call such a beautiful spot that?"

"Historically, when people left to emigrate to other countries, they caught the coach here that would take them to the port and their boat. In most cases, their families knew they would never see them again."

"Oh, that's so sad."

Mick hesitated, not sure where to start with what he really wanted to say.

"Mick, what happens to us?" Carrie asked softly. She leaned against the bridge with her back to the water.

"Carrie, I'm not husband material," he said. "You've seen that yourself these last ten years."

"It sounds like you've already made up your mind."

Mick listed the cons for her: the distance and her career and his inability to move.

Carrie folded her arms across her chest and appeared thoughtful, listening to everything he said. When he was finished, she asked, "Is that all?"

Mick stared down at his shoes.

"Mick?"

Finally, he looked up at her. "My father was a horrible man. He was a terrible husband and father. I watched for years as he belittled my mother and made her cry," he said through gritted teeth. "And I swore to myself that I would never treat another person like he did, especially a woman." He paused before saying softly, "Women are so amazing in their own right; they're meant to be loved, adored, and cherished. But no matter how much I believe this, I still have my father's genes in me."

"You can't be serious," Carrie protested.

"I have already hurt you once, and I can barely forgive myself for that," Mick said.

"But I've forgiven you!" she said.

"I couldn't bear it if I turned into my father," he said.

"You can't judge your future on someone else's past!" she cried. "I didn't know your father, but you are a kind and good man."

"I'm sorry, Carrie," he said.

"Wait a minute!" Carrie said. "You've made decisions here about our future. And not once have you asked me what I want. You just assumed. And yet despite these excuses—and that's just what they are—you haven't once mentioned how you feel about me."

Mick remained silent. If he started on his feelings, it might undo everything.

"Do you know why I married you?" she asked.

"To help me stay in the country," he replied.

"Besides that," she said. "I married you because I had fallen in love with you, and I hoped that someday you would feel the same way about me."

As difficult as it was, Mick didn't say anything, thinking he was doing Carrie a favor in the long run.

Carrie reached out to touch the side of his face but changed her mind. Her fingers curled into her palm, and she withdrew her hand.

"Goodbye, Mick," she said in a strangled voice, her eyes full of tears. She turned on her heel and left him.

He'd been right. He'd made a woman cry; he was just like his father after all.

CHAPTER NINETEEN

CARRIE HAD PULLED HERSELF together by the following morning. She'd accepted her fate; she didn't like it, but she had resigned herself to it. When she got home, she would seek a divorce.

The last interview Carrie had scheduled was in the afternoon before the crowning of the King and Queen of Kilcornan later that evening at McAllister's dance hall.

She walked over to the Bridge of Tears—aptly named, she thought—where she'd agreed to meet Steven and Betty McInerney, a couple who'd been married twenty years and had been set up by Mick's mother.

She threw up her hand in a wave to the couple.

"Steven! Betty!" Her voice cracked in greeting. *Pull yourself together and be the professional that you are!* she chastised herself. *Leave your personal affairs out of it.*

"We thought you'd forgotten about us," Betty said with a laugh.

"Oh no," Carrie said. "I'm just running a bit behind. I'm sorry."

"No worries," Betty said. She seemed to be studying Carrie, and her features flooded with concern.

"Are you all right, Carrie?" Steven asked. "Your face is all blotchy. And your eyes are red." Betty gave him a harsh elbow to the ribs and Steve stooped over slightly, emitting a soft "Oomph."

"I found a lovely place down by the river where we can sit and chat," Betty said. She looked up to the sky and announced, "It's such a beautiful day I thought it might be nicer if we sat outside."

Carrie wanted to throw her arms around Betty in gratitude for the distraction of the weather. Carrie nodded, and the three of them walked along the river, through the park, until they found an empty picnic table.

The trees in the park were big and green and leafy. A few benches and picnic tables painted green and white dotted the small space. The river was narrow and shallow where it edged along the one side of the park, but it appeared turbulent. The sound of rushing water could be heard throughout the park.

Steven and Betty were from County Kilkenny. Steven worked as a bank manager, and Betty worked as a primary-school teacher.

Once they sat down at the picnic table, Carrie flipped her notebook open to a new page and uncapped her pen.

"It was Mrs. Foley who arranged your match?" Carrie started.

Betty nodded. "In those days, you didn't fill out forms, and there was nothing online. You drove up to Kilcornan during the off-season—"

"Off-season?" Carrie repeated.

"All the rest of the year when the festival wasn't on," Steven explained.

"I had an appointment with Mrs. Foley and spent an hour in conversation with her. She was a lovely woman. Real tall, just like her daughter, Rosemary. But gentle, with a wicked sense of humor. And a great baker. Her scones were divine," Betty said with a heavenward sigh.

Carrie waited for Betty to finish her recollection of the events that brought her and her husband together.

"Anyway, after the interview, she told me she'd be in contact with me." Betty laughed. "I went home thinking I'd hear from her in a day or two, but she didn't ring. Three months later, I phoned her to see if anything was happening. Mrs. Foley laughed and said, 'It's not like I can walk down to the shop and pick up a husband for you. These things take time, as long as they need to,'" Betty recalled, looking at her husband. "I didn't hear from her for another six months. Then one day, she rang me out of the blue and said that she had a nice fella for me and wanted to know if I'd be able to come up that weekend."

"And did you?"

Betty nodded. "I did. And I met Steven, and we've been together ever since."

Their happy-ending story made Carrie feel like she wanted to cry. Everybody else's story seemed to have a happy ending except her own.

"Steven, was that your first time visiting a matchmaker?"

Steven nodded. "Yes, and I told no one. But once I met Betty, I told everyone!"

They laughed.

"I was almost thirty when I resorted to the services of a matchmaker. All my friends were getting married and starting families, and I wanted that for myself—someone to go through life's ups and downs with." Here Steven paused and looked fondly at his wife, who smiled at him. "I wasn't one for hanging out in the pubs to meet people; it just wasn't my thing. So I made an appointment with the matchmaker. The funny thing is, Mrs. Foley never took a note or wrote anything down during our meeting."

"You wonder how she managed to keep everyone straight without writing anything down," Carrie said.

Betty chimed in. "She said she never forgot a face or the personality that went along with it."

"Did she ever explain the secrets to her success?" Carrie asked.

"I asked her that once, and her answer was vague," Betty said with a funny smile. "She said she just knew."

Hmm, like mother, like son, Carrie thought to herself. Not wanting to think about Mick, she returned her focus to the couple in front of her. Carrie glanced at her notes. "And you've been together now for twenty years? And you have kids?"

"We've got four kids. Three daughters and a son," Steve said proudly.

"But it hasn't always been smooth sailing," Betty said seriously.

Carrie looked at her, then at Steven, then back to Betty. Steven looked at his wife with a gentle smile and then looked down at the table but said nothing.

"What do you mean?" Carrie asked, looking for clarification.

"We hit a rough patch eight years in and separated for a year," Betty divulged.

Steven looked at his wife again with the same smile and drummed his fingers on the table. He remained silent, and Carrie wondered if the past still held painful memories for him.

"The initial passion from the early years had waned," Betty explained, "and we kind of drifted apart."

Steve finally spoke up. "There wasn't any one big issue that caused the split. We just needed a break to recalibrate."

Betty looked over at him and smiled at him lovingly. "Steve always says that about that year of separation, that we just needed to 'recalibrate.' I just love that word."

"Obviously, it worked out, as you're here today."

"We did a lot of counseling," Steve said. "At the beginning of any new relationship, the passion is high, but those kinds of intense emotions are difficult to sustain over any length of time. If you're lucky, that blaze of passion dies down to a strong ember, and what you're left with is something very deep and very rich." Steve reached out and placed his hand over Betty's, and she smiled and squeezed his hand. "But the most important thing is forgiveness. You can't go forward until you forgive all the hurts and the slights."

Betty added, "Forgive, forgive, forgive."

Carrie wondered if she'd ever have anything like that in her life. Mick had probably been the greatest love of her life. She couldn't see anyone ever taking his place. But all she had was a marriage in name only. And pretty soon, she wouldn't even have that.

A bird twittered overhead, and the sun beat down on Carrie's face.

She thanked the McInerneys for their time and their willingness to talk to her on the record. She shook their hands and watched as they walked off together, hand in hand, a picture of domestic bliss even after a breakup.

One more day and then she could go home. She was ready.

Chapter Twenty

Mick was in his office when Rosemary appeared in the doorway. He was just wrapping up things for the day. He had purposely kept busy all day, from talking to everyone he met to cleaning out all the drawers in his file cabinets in his office. He'd swapped out sad Irish music for rousing pub songs. He'd washed the baseboards and cleaned the windows of his office and the café. Tonight was the last night of the festival, and he still had to choose a couple for the King and Queen of Kilcornan.

Mick carried his empty teacup and plate from lunch to the kitchen.

Rosemary worked quietly on the other side of the kitchen.

His sister stopped what she was doing. Her white apron was covered in stains and flour. Her dark hair was covered with a red-flowered kerchief. Standing there with her hands on her hips, Rosemary looked formidable.

"Did you talk to Carrie?" she asked. "She's leaving tomorrow, isn't she?"

"We're going our separate ways," he said, not in the mood. He had purposely kept busy so he wouldn't have to think about Carrie or what he had done.

"What? Whose decision was this? Yours or hers?" she asked. Mick did not miss the annoyance in her voice.

"It was mine. It's for the best."

"Oh, you flippin' eejit!" Rosemary yelled, startling Mick. "Are you for real? Or are you that stupid?"

"Probably all of the above," Mick answered.

"Don't be flip!" she said. "For the past two weeks, the whole town has watched the two of you staring at each other like a couple of lovesick cows!"

"Was it that obvious?" Mick asked.

Rosemary rolled her eyes. "Yes, it was. The space station even rang and asked if the two of you had figured it out yet." She paused and exhaled loudly, unable to hide her disgust for her younger brother. "Why do you think Sarah, Maeve, Millie, and myself went to all the trouble to sign you both up for all those activities?"

"You were all in on this together?" Mick asked.

"Of course, you fool! You both needed a push—no, a shove. And you've gone and blown it. Do not let that girl leave this country without making this right. You are making a big mistake in letting her go, and you'll regret it for the rest of your life."

Mick was about to protest and tell his sister to mind her own business when they were interrupted by the sound of the back door opening, followed by a bellow.

"Rosemary!" It was Dennis.

Rosemary quickly pulled off her kerchief and smoothed back her hair, her countenance softening.

Dennis appeared in the kitchen, and his face broke into a smile at the sight of Rosemary.

Rosemary tripped over something and immediately reddened. "Hello, Dennis."

"How're you keeping?" Dennis asked.

"I'm well, how about you?" she asked.

Mick rolled his eyes, wondering how long the two of them were going to dance around each other. It was getting to the point where it was painful. And she had the nerve to talk about him and Carrie.

"I've got the order. I've also got some nice end-of-the-season rhubarb for you. Don't tell anyone. I told my other customers that we were all out."

Rosemary blushed. She rounded on Mick. "Don't you have a king and queen to crown?"

"I do." He paused before his sister and Dennis. They looked at him expectantly.

"The two of you are pathetic," he said with emphasis, and pointed to his sister. Dennis seemed taken aback by Mick's bluntness.

Rosemary's eyes widened as she warned, "Mick . . ."

"I've watched for the last year as the two of you steal glances at each other. One or the other blushes. Dennis gives you all sorts of one-of-a-kind specials that he's giving no one else. And you, Rosemary, always have a cup of tea, a sandwich, and a piece of cake ready for Dennis every Tuesday." Mick looked at the produce man. "No other vendor coming through here gets that. They don't even get a cup of tea."

Dennis looked at Rosemary. "Is that true, Rosemary?"

Rosemary cast her eyes downward and nodded, playing with the hem of her apron.

Dennis looked at Mick and said, "Would you excuse us, Mick? What I have to say to your sister is for her ears only." Dennis reached for her hand, and Rosemary covered her eyes with her other hand.

As he was walking out the door, he heard Dennis ask softly, "Why are you crying, Rosemary?"

Mick closed the door behind him, smiling. At least one of them should be happy.

Mick headed over to McAllister's dance hall. Although it was still early, it was packed, and the dancing was in full swing. Mick stayed in the background, away from Carrie. But just because he stayed out of sight didn't mean he didn't know where she was at all times. She and Kathy stood on the periphery, watching the dancing.

Rosemary and Dennis soon joined them. They were holding hands, and Mick smiled.

"Good band," Dennis said to Rosemary.

"It is," she said, looking at everything and everyone but him.

"Would you dance with me, Rosemary?" Dennis asked.

Rosemary looked down at him, their height difference notable, and she was about to protest but Dennis cut her off with a grin. "I don't mind if you don't mind."

Before Rosemary could protest any further, Dennis led her by the hand to the dance floor. "Come on, Rosemary, you can even lead if you want to."

A smile tugged at the corners of Rosemary's mouth.

Mick had never seen his sister on any dance floor as she usually avoided these social situations. Back in secondary school, her height had peaked at six feet and unfortunately, she hadn't only been taller than all the girls in her class but the boys as well, including those in the upper classes. Social situations like these where you needed a partner had left her feeling excluded. Although she was very attractive, some men just couldn't look past her impossible height.

Good on you, Dennis, Mick thought.

"Hey, Mick, how are you?" Marie asked.

"Hi, Marie." Mick smiled. As usual, she was on her own. He didn't ask where Jim was because he had a pretty good idea. Instead, they made small talk, and he was thankful for the conversation as it took his mind off his hopeless situation with Carrie.

The band played a lively number and Mick turned to Marie. "Would you like to dance?"

"I'd love to!" she enthused.

As he twirled her around the dance floor, she said, "I love dancing, but Jim doesn't, so that's that."

Mick wanted to say something, but he bit his tongue.

Marie appeared to be enjoying herself and once she relaxed, she seemed to Mick about ten years younger.

They were in the middle of the fourth set, and Mick was thinking how he could use a beverage. He'd kept his eye on Carrie the entire time, wishing she would look in his direction. He was beginning to second-guess his decision. Maybe Rosemary was right. Maybe he was a fool.

He was about to spin Marie around when he felt a tap on his shoulder. Turning around, he came face to face with a fist from Jim, Marie's husband.

The pain was unreal, and Mick swore he saw stars as he went reeling back.

"Keep away from my wife!" Jim shouted. The dance floor came to a standstill and there were shouts of astonishment.

Paul came charging over and said to Jim, "You're coming with me down to the garda station. Mick, did you want to press charges?"

Mick, now leaning against a table, shook his head. "No, I don't." He didn't want to embarrass Marie, although suddenly she was nowhere to be seen.

"Where's Marie?" Jim shouted.

But his shouting fell on deaf ears as he was escorted from McAllister's. The dancing had yet to resume, and Mick looked up and saw Carrie across the dance floor with her hands to her mouth, watching him.

Marie reappeared with ice cubes wrapped in a towel. She laid the ice pack gently across Mick's cheek and eye.

"Here, this will help decrease the swelling," Marie said.

Mick hoped she didn't know that from personal experience. "Will you step outside with me for some fresh air?" he asked her.

Marie nodded and said as they exited the dance hall, "Mick, I am so sorry. He's so excitable."

Certifiable was a better word.

Mick leaned against the wall, holding the towel-wrapped ice cubes against his face. Mick had purposely led her out the back, behind McAllister's, so they could talk in private.

Marie stood there, arms folded across her chest, her head lowered and her eyes darting about.

"Marie, I don't usually interfere, but I'm going to say my piece," Mick started.

Marie's eyes grew round, and she froze to the spot.

"I won't presume to know how Jim acts at home, but if he treats you like this in public then chances are, he's treating you much worse at home. And frankly, that is just not on."

Marie bit her bottom lip, and her chin quivered.

"If he's never told you before then I'm going to tell you: you are a wonderful human being who deserves so much better."

Marie nodded but said nothing. She looked as if she was fighting back tears.

"Here's the thing, Marie," Mick said with a sigh. "You've got young boys in the house. Don't let your sons grow up thinking that this is how women are to be treated."

"But divorce . . ." she said, her voice trailing off.

"I'm not saying go home and get a divorce. But get into counseling. Both of you. Try to fix it before you start calling solicitors."

Marie spoke with a quivering voice. "You've been very kind to me, Mick."

Mick looked at her with a gentle smile. "My mother was in the same situation as you. She stayed with my father until he died but never knew a moment's peace in her marriage." It was something he never spoke of publicly, his parents' difficult marriage and his father's drinking. But if he could help someone in the way he wished he had helped his mother, then he would do it.

Marie seemed to process this.

The ice began to melt, and Mick unraveled the towel and threw what was left of the ice on the ground.

"I'd better get down to the garda station and see what's going on with Jim," Marie said. She extended her hand. "Thank you."

Mick shook it and watched her walk off. Once she disappeared, he headed back into the dance hall. The crowning of the King and Queen of Kilcornan was at the end of the evening, and he still didn't know who he was picking. He hoped some inspiration appeared soon.

He decided his sister was right, and the urge to talk to Carrie was overwhelming. He approached Carrie and Kathy. He could feel his eye beginning to swell shut.

"Carrie, will you dance with me?" he asked, his voice choked with emotion.

Carrie shook her head, and her chin quivered. "No."

"Come on, I'll dance with you," Kathy said. "I want to talk to you anyway."

Carrie looked aghast. Before Mick could protest, Kathy dragged him out to the dance floor.

Chapter Twenty-One

CARRIE THOUGHT SHE WAS hallucinating when she caught a glimpse of Kathy's boyfriend, David, barreling through the dance hall. Frantically, she searched the dance floor for Kathy and Mick. They were at the other end. She needed to reach them and separate them before David did.

Carrie pushed her way through the crowd of moving couples on the dance floor using her elbows and her shoulders. As she shoved, she tried to spy David, but she'd lost sight of him. He had chosen to skirt around the edges of the dance floor.

Mick and Kathy remained unaware of David's presence. They looked to be in the middle of a serious conversation, and Carrie knew that David would misconstrue that.

She was within arm's reach of Kathy when she spotted David tapping Kathy on her shoulder. Kathy turned around, and her smile morphed into a look of surprise and then back to a broad smile again. She looked happy to see him. Mick looked wary. And David looked furious.

Carrie dashed toward the three of them to head off what she suspected was going to be a cataclysm.

"Is this the guy you've been seeing behind my back?" David shouted.

Some of the other dancers stopped mid-step to see what all the commotion was about.

"No!" Kathy yelled. "Don't be ridiculous!"

The band stopped playing.

Mick went to put up his hand to explain, but David knocked it away with his right. Carrie knew what was coming next, and she lunged for David but missed. David swung his left fist and it connected with Mick's face. Mick's head snapped back, and he teetered before falling on the floor. As he went to get up with eyes that were dark and an expression that was stormy, Carrie ran to him and knelt by him on the ground.

"Oh, Mick!" she cried.

Mick wobbled and said, "It's just not my day." He attempted to sit up.

"Please don't," she whispered. "It will only make things worse."

He rubbed his chin and moved his jaw back and forth, trying to see if it was broken. Carrie pulled him into her lap. His dark expression was replaced with a look of surprise.

"Only for you," he said through gritted teeth. "Or else I'd knock him right into the middle of next week."

"Thank you," she murmured. She pushed his hair off his forehead, and his expression softened.

David bent over Mick. "My name's David Keller, I'm a detective in the Philadelphia police department, robbery division. And I'm going to tell you the same thing I tell all my perps. You don't take what doesn't belong to you. Got it?"

Kathy yelled, "David, are you crazy?"

David cast a glance at Mick to make sure he wasn't going to retaliate, and rubbed the back of his head. "Maybe I am, Kathy.

But I've been crazy since you left. When you first left, I thought it was going to be great. No more nagging. I could eat pizza and drink beer and watch a basketball, football, or baseball game without any interruptions."

Kathy folded her arms across her chest. Her eyes filled with tears. "Well, now you won't have to worry about me interrupting ever again."

David shook his head. "No, babe, I'm not finished."

"I'm listening," she said.

Carrie and Mick, as well as everyone else on the dance floor, watched the unfolding drama between Kathy and David.

"Yeah, I thought it would be great. I'll admit it. But after twenty-four hours it was awful. You know what's great?" he asked.

"No, what? Two for one at the corner bar?" Kathy asked with a smirk.

David laughed. "You got me there. But no, here's what's great: Coming home to you every night. Just knowing that you're there for me. You know what else is great? We both know that in being with you, I've moved up in the world. You're out of my league. I'm not good enough for you. I know it. You know it. Everyone knows it. Doesn't your father remind me regularly?"

That drew some laughs from those within earshot.

"And despite this, you still love me. Sometimes I think about that, and it just blows my mind. You could have had anyone you wanted, and yet you picked me."

Kathy looked at him, confused. "You think about that?"

"I do," he said. "I'm glad you left me."

"You are?" she asked, confusion plain on her face.

Carrie was starting to get confused herself at this point. She suddenly realized she'd been holding Mick and brushing his hair off his forehead absentmindedly as she watched David and Kathy. She looked at him, reddened, and said, "Oh, sorry, I didn't realize what I was doing."

She pulled her hand away, but he whispered, never taking his eyes off her, "Don't stop."

She looked down, smiled at him, and ran her fingers through his hair once more. They turned their attention back to Kathy and David.

"Yeah, you leaving me was the wake-up call I needed," David admitted. "Kath, I just don't work without you. I'm no good, babe. It's as simple as that."

"I just feel we're in a rut," Kathy said. Her eyes were full of tears that threatened to spill.

David nodded. "We are. And I'm willing to do whatever it takes to save our relationship."

"You just don't listen to me," Kathy countered.

"I admit I do need to work on that, but sometimes you don't give me credit," David said.

"How do you mean?" Kathy asked.

"Because sometimes I do listen."

"Really?" Kathy asked.

"Yeah. I do. And I do more than that."

"Prove it."

"Okay. You know that woman you work with? Betsy? The one you can't stand?"

"Yeah," Kathy said, unsure where this was going.

"Do you know why you don't like her?"

"Because she's annoying?" Kathy said.

"Nah, babe, it's because you admire her. You have a girl crush on her, and she doesn't give you the time of day."

Kathy didn't hide her outrage. "I most certainly do not!"

"Listen, Kath, I'm a detective. I get paid to observe."

"Well, I disagree," she huffed. "What else?"

"One of your favorite things is your first cup of coffee of the day. You love rain and wind because they help you sleep. As soon as you get home from work, you take off your bra."

There was a ripple of laughter in the crowd, and Kathy's face turned the color of puce.

Kathy's lips thinned. "You couldn't think of anything else? You had to put that out there for public consumption?"

David grinned. "Hey, babe, I'm not complaining." He winked at her, and the crowd laughed louder.

"David!" Kathy protested, but even she couldn't help but smile. "Okay, anything else?"

"Yes." David smiled. He reached into his back pocket and pulled out his wallet. "I want to show you something." He opened his wallet and pulled something out. "Do you remember when you showed me this?"

Kathy frowned, not knowing what it was.

David opened up a folded page that had been torn from a magazine. The gloss had dulled, and there were creases in the paper where it had been folded and tucked away in his wallet for a while.

"You said it was your dream ring," David said, opening it up.

Kathy's hands flew to her mouth. "You saved that?"

It was David's turn to look offended. "Of course I did. Why do you think I've been doing all this overtime for the last three years?"

"It is a ring I would love, but I don't expect you to pay that kind of money for a ring."

David laughed. "I wish you would have told me that before I started saving for it." He pulled a small box from his pocket, got down on one knee, and held the box out to her.

"Kathy, love of my life, will you marry me?" he asked.

Tears streamed down Kathy's face. "David, that's your bad knee you're kneeling on!"

"Not the response I was hoping for!" he joked. Carrie and Mick laughed along with all the other onlookers.

Kathy reached forward and placed her hands on the sides of David's face and laughed. "Yes! I'll marry you!" And she pulled him up to her as the crowd around them erupted in cheers.

With tears in her own eyes, Carrie sighed. "I love a good romance."

She looked down at Mick to find he was staring at her. He reached up and tucked a stray lock of hair behind her ear. "Me, too," he said softly.

His eyes glittered in the semi-light of the dance hall. He whispered, "Kiss me, Mrs. Foley."

Carrie's lips parted ever so slightly as she leaned down to kiss him.

But they were interrupted by David.

"You still on the floor, bud? Sorry about that," David said.

"Am I still on the floor?" Mick said. "I hadn't noticed."

Carrie, still on her knees, pulled back and straightened her spine, embarrassed.

"No hard feelings, I hope," David said to Mick as he reached out to help him up. "But Kathy's my woman. Get your own."

Once Mick was up off the floor, he reached down and held his hand out for Carrie.

David grinned. "I see you've already moved on."

Carrie placed her hand in Mick's.

Chapter Twenty-Two

M ICK SUSPECTED THAT BY morning, his face would be a map of bruises and he'd be sporting a pair of black eyes. What a night! They stood at the edge of the dance floor, Carrie's hand still in his.

The band began playing again, and couples went back to dancing. Mick recognized the song immediately: "When You Were Sweet Sixteen." He swallowed hard, choking down the feelings that welled up within him. It was a song that reminded him of when he first met Carrie.

"Dance with me," he said to her. His eyes glistened in the low lighting of the ballroom.

Carrie laughed. "Now? I was going to get you some ice and a cup of tea."

He shook his head. "I don't need that. I *need* you to dance this song with me. Just one song." He was going to try to right a wrong, starting now.

Before she could answer or protest, he led her by the hand onto the dance floor, slipping into the midst of the throng of other couples. When he took her into his arms, he held her close, marveling at the feel of her body against his. He rested his hurt chin against her hair, breathing her in. He closed his eyes with a sigh, and they moved together in time to the music. It had taken more than ten years for him to get her into his arms. His thoughts were a kaleidoscope of images: the past when they were young, these last two weeks, and their future.

"This song always reminds me of you," he said, his voice a whisper against her ear.

She frowned. "It does?"

"Always," he replied. "Whenever I hear it, I think of those few weeks we had together."

"You thought about that?" she asked, looking up at him with a quizzical expression.

"All the time."

He danced her slowly around the dance floor for the remainder of the song, holding her close, lost in the moment. When it was over, the need to be alone with her overwhelmed him, and he led her off the dance floor and outside to a private place.

"Do you remember when you offered to marry me?" he asked.

"Of course I do," she replied. She leaned against the wall of the dance hall.

"You never asked me why I wanted to stay in the US," he said.

Carrie shrugged and frowned in confusion, unsure of what he was saying. "I just thought it was because you liked America so much."

Mick shook his head. "I loved America, but the reason I wanted to stay was you."

"Me?" she repeated, blinking.

Mick lowered his voice. "I didn't want to leave you. Not when I was falling in love with you."

"Oh." Carrie stared at him, open-mouthed.

Mick figured he might as well say it all. Get it out there. "The day I married you, I loved you. The day I left, I loved you. I have never stopped loving you," Mick said.

"You love me?" Carrie asked, incredulous. Tears filled her eyes. "I offered to marry you because I was falling in love with you!"

Mick grinned. Rosemary was right. "We're nothing but a pair of eejits!"

"I thought you were afraid. With your father and stuff," she said.

"I am afraid. But I don't want to be anymore. I don't want to miss out on anything with you."

Tears fell from Carrie's eyes. "We've lost all this time, Mick!" she cried.

Mick stepped next to her and pulled her quickly into his arms, whispering into her ear. "Shh. None of that matters. It worked out the way it was supposed to. We start right here, right now. Forgive me."

He thought for a moment. Maybe he shouldn't assume anything. "That's if you want to, Carrie."

She nodded quickly, wiping the tears from her eyes.

He breathed a sigh of relief. "Remember that last day, the day we were supposed to go on that picnic?" It had been the worst day of his life. He'd lost both his mother and his wife. From his pocket, he pulled a slim gold wedding band. "I had planned on giving you this at the picnic."

Carrie's hands flew to her mouth. "Oh, Mick!"

"I'd like you to have it," Mick said.

"I'd like to wear it," Carrie said softly.

Mick nodded, feeling more pleased than he had in a long time. He held out his hand and she placed her left hand in his. As he slipped the band on her ring finger, he whispered, "This is for life, Mrs. Foley."

She nodded and threw her arms around his neck. He slid his arms around her waist, pulled her closer and kissed her.

"There you are!" Rosemary said, interrupting them.

Mick and Carrie pulled their lips apart but stayed in each other's arms.

"It looks like you've got everything sorted," Rosemary said.

When Mick nodded, she said, "Good. Welcome to the family, Carrie."

"Thanks, Rosemary," Carrie said shyly.

"Not to interrupt, but they're looking for you to crown the king and the queen," Rosemary said.

"I'll be there soon," he said, and he looked at Carrie. "I want five more minutes with my wife."

Mick took the stage with Carrie at his side, her hand in his.

"It's that time of year again," Mick announced. "When we crown the couple to be King and Queen Kilcornan!"

"What about you and your American girlfriend?" someone shouted from the crowd.

Mick laughed, looked over at Carrie, and gave her hand a gentle, reassuring squeeze. "No, that would hardly be fair. As the town's matchmaker, I'm disqualified from partaking."

A wave of *aws* spread through the crowd.

"But no worries, we've got a good king and queen this year," he said. "The last two weeks, I was having a hard time choosing.

There are just so many lovely couples out there this year, and we wish you the best of luck in your romance."

There were murmurs of "you, too!" from the mass of people.

"Let me just say again, it wasn't easy to decide. There were so many high-quality candidates for King and Queen. I decided to just trust the process, as they say, believing that the right couple would present themselves." He paused. "And then suddenly, it came out of nowhere, literally, and all I can say is that it involved a wicked left hook."

Everybody laughed.

"Anyway, without further ado, I'd like to present to you the King and Queen of Kilcornan." He turned to Carrie on the stage and said into the microphone, "Carrie, would you call up our new king and queen?"

Carrie took the microphone from Mick and with a broad smile, she announced, "Let's welcome the new King and Queen of Kilcornan, David Keller and Kathy McClintock!"

There were whoops as the winning couple made their way toward the stage. David held Kathy's hand and smiled. "Settle down, settle down," he said in his usual blustery manner. David and Kathy ascended the steps to the platform, and Mick led them to their thrones.

David kissed Kathy on the mouth and said, "I always told you that you were a queen, babe."

They sat on their thrones and Mick placed a decoupage crown on Kathy's head while Carrie placed one on David's.

"If I'd known Ireland was going to be this much fun, I would have come over sooner," David said.

EPILOGUE

TWO YEARS LATER

I T WAS A SUNNY June day. Carrie stepped outside the Caherdavin Arms in her wedding gown. Her mother and her
sister fussed over her, adjusting her veil and train.

"You look beautiful, darling," her mother smiled, her eyes
full of tears.

"No crying, Mom, you'll ruin your make-up," her older
sister, Trish laughed. Carrie's dress was a simple affair of ivory
satin with a lace overlay. Mick had gifted her with a diamond
bandeau, which now held her veil in place and glittered in the
afternoon sun.

Her father looked on proudly. "Everything looks perfect."

Kathy and David emerged from the hotel with Sarah.

"Oh Carrie!" Kathy said, her eyes full of tears. Her own
wedding set sparkled on her left hand. Her face went pale. "I'm
so sorry," she cried, as she leaned behind a shrub and threw up.

They all looked on in sympathy. Kathy was three months
pregnant and despite morning sickness, had insisted on traveling over for Carrie's wedding.

David appeared out of nowhere, his face a picture of concern. "Kath! Babe! You all right?" he asked, as he put his arm around her and rubbed her back. She stood up, took the handkerchief that David offered and wiped her mouth. Little flecks of mascara dotted beneath her eyes.

Viewing the mess behind the shrub, Kathy groaned. "Oh Sarah, I'm so sorry."

Sarah went to say something, but David cut her off. "Sarah, I'll clean that up." He looked at Kathy tenderly. "After all, it's my kid that caused that mess." This drew a smile from Kathy. David kissed her forehead. Laughing, he said, "You know, Kath, I wonder if this kid is going to be a troublemaker like his old man!"

This elicited another groan from Kathy, and the rest of them laughed.

Maeve and Millie O'Donovan came toward Carrie. Each wore a formal dress and a matching hat with some kind of floral arrangement. Maeve's dress was a deep blue and Millie's was lavender. They reminded Carrie of a pair of hydrangeas.

Maeve handed Carrie a small, faded blue silk purse. "This was our mother's when she married our Da. We're giving it to you. Inside is a shiny new coin."

"For something borrowed, something blue, something old and something new," Millie explained.

Carrie thanked them and held the purse with her bouquet.

"Come on, Millie, we need to get to the church!"

Carrie was happy. And she had the people she loved most around her to celebrate the happiest day of her life.

She stepped out into the road to begin her walk up to the church at the top of the town. The church would be full with her family and friends that had flown over from the States as well Mick's family and friends and townspeople.

At the matchmaking festival the previous April, Carrie and Mick had announced their upcoming church wedding. They'd started a mailing list of anyone who wanted to attend the wedding. The response had been overwhelming.

Carrie looked up the beautifully decorated street, strung with the familiar red-and-white bunting and lights, and lined with red and white petunias and geraniums.

"Will we get this show on the road?" her father asked, with a clap of his hands.

"You know, I think I'd like to walk up the road to the church," Carrie said, looking up at the cloudless, blue sky.

"We can all walk," her father said.

"I'm going to drive Kath up to the church," David said.

"No, David, I want to walk with her," Kathy said.

"You're the boss. Let's go."

Carrie, clutching her bouquet of red and white roses, began to walk up the street. On each side of her were her parents. Kathy, David, and Sarah walked behind them. She wanted to enjoy her day, looking at all the decorations. Townspeople walked ahead of her, and soon word traveled that the bride was on foot to the church. The crowd gradually stepped aside to each side of the street to allow the bride through.

Marie stood by herself on the footpath. She waved to Carrie and smiled. Her husband had refused counseling, and Marie had summoned the courage to leave him before Christmas. Mick had told Carrie that when Marie was ready, he was going to find her a perfect match. Carrie hoped so.

She admired all the shop windows adorned with fairy lights and decorations for her wedding. She understood why people came back every year. She never wanted to leave.

As they passed the newspaper offices, Carrie was filled with pride. They'd purchased the paper, and Carrie worked doing what she'd come to love best: the human-interest stories of Kilcornan.

Carrie was overcome with emotion when she spotted Mick standing outside the café. In a simple, elegant black suit with a white shirt and tie and a single white rosebud for a boutonniere, he looked so handsome he took her breath away. Like her, he was beaming.

He stood with Rosemary and Dennis. Both grinned from ear to ear; their own wedding was scheduled for the autumn.

Mick stepped off the footpath and reached for her and took her hand in his.

"You look stunning!" he whispered.

Carrie lowered her eyes, pleased. "You don't think it's bad luck for the groom to see the bride before the ceremony?"

Mick shook his head, smiling. "Nope."

He kissed her mother on the cheek and shook her father's hand.

The crowd around them, lining the sidewalks, broke into shouts and cheers as Carrie and Mick strolled, hand in hand, to the church, ready to get married. Again.

Carrie caught a glimpse of Breda Horan. John had passed away six months earlier, and Carrie and Mick had gone to the wake and funeral. Jerry and Margaret Mullane stood with their two-year-old daughter. Margaret—again—was due any day.

Paul, the garda, power-walked by them, stopping briefly to wish them well. From behind they heard the voice of Charlotte Connors.

"Paul, wait up!" she called.

Paul cringed and said to Mick, "How did you get rid of Charlotte?"

Mick smiled and gave Carrie's hand a squeeze. "I got married to someone else."

Paul wiped his brow and said, "That seems a little extreme." He went off in the direction of the church with Charlotte gaining on him, her dress vibrant colors of red, orange, and purple, resembling the plumage of some rare, exotic tropical bird. She waved to them as she ran past, wishing them luck.

When they reached the church doors, David threw them open and with a quick peek inside, Carrie saw that all the pews were filled. The parish priest, Father Burke, waited at the end of the center aisle, standing in front of the altar.

Mick turned to Carrie and took both her hands in his. "Are you ready?"

Carrie squeezed his hands, feeling surer and more confident about this than she ever had about anything in her life. She nodded, smiling. "Let's do this!"

Mick looked around, aware of all eyes on them. "May I kiss the bride first?"

Carrie giggled. "Please."

He leaned down to her and Carrie closed her eyes, her lips parting in anticipation, her heart beginning to hammer against her chest.

She never tired of his kiss. And they'd done a lot of kissing over the last two years.

When he pulled away, he smiled a dream-like smile at her. "I'm looking forward to spending the rest of my life with you."

Carrie smiled wide. "Me, too."

He regarded her thoughtfully. "Are you happy?"

She nodded. "You?"

"Yes, very." He held her hand and stepped forward into the church. "Come on my love, it's time to get married."

NOTE

ALSO BY MICHELE BROUDER

Coming in 2026

The Gallagher Brothers of Galway Bay
Fake Dating, Irish Style

Escape to Ireland
A Match Made in Ireland
Her Fake Irish Husband
Her Irish Inheritance
A Match for the Matchmaker
Home, Sweet Irish Home
An Irish Christmas

Happy Holidays
A Whyte Christmas
This Christmas
A Wish for Christmas
One Kiss for Christmas

A Wedding for Christmas

Hideaway Bay
Coming Home to Hideaway Bay
Meet Me at Sunrise
Moonlight and Promises
When We Were Young
One Last Thing Before I Go
The Chocolatier of Hideaway Bay
Now and Forever

The Lavender Bay Chronicles
The Inn at Lavender Bay
Lost and Found in Lavender Bay
Second Chances in Lavender Bay
New Beginnings in Lavender Bay
Looking Back in Lavender Bay
Sisters and Friends in Lavender Bay

Soul Saver Series
Claire Daly: Reluctant Soul Saver
Claire Daly: Marked for Collection

*All romance and women's fiction titles are available in ebook,
paperback, and large print paperback. Audiobooks are currently
being rolled out.*

9 781914 476174